Published in 2021 by Groundwood Books / House of Anansi Press
groundwoodbooks.com

Groundwood Books respectfully acknowledges that the land on
which we operate is the Traditional Territory of many Nations,
including the Anishinabeg, the Wendat and the Haudenosaunee.
It is also the Treaty Lands of the Mississaugas of the Credit.

We gratefully acknowledge for their financial support of our
publishing program the Canada Council for the Arts, the Ontario
Arts Council and the Government of Canada.

Canada Council   Conseil des Arts
for the Arts   du Canada

ONTARIO ARTS COUNCIL
CONSEIL DES ARTS DE L'ONTARIO
an Ontario government agency
un organisme du gouvernement de l'Ontario

With the participation of the Government of Canada   Canadä
Avec la participation du gouvernement du Canada

Library and Archives Canada Cataloguing in Publication
Title: Anthony and the gargoyle / story by Jo Ellen Bogart ;
pictures by Maja Kastelic.
Names: Bogart, Jo Ellen, author. | Kastelic, Maja, illustrator.
Identifiers: Canadiana (print) 20200388754 | Canadiana
(ebook) 20200388762 | ISBN 9781773063447 (hardcover) | ISBN
9781773063454 (EPUB) | ISBN 9781773063461 (Kindle)
Classification: LCC PS8553.O465 A78 2021 | DDC jC813/.54—dc23

The illustrations were painted with gouache, then colored digitally.
Design by Michael Solomon and Lucia Kim
Printed and bound in South Korea

FSC
MIX
Paper from
responsible sources
FSC® C013572

To Sheila — JEB

For G, my restless wanderer — MK

Anthony
and the
Gargoyle

Story by

Jo Ellen Bogart

Pictures by

Maja Kastelic

GROUNDWOOD BOOKS
HOUSE OF ANANSI PRESS
TORONTO / BERKELEY

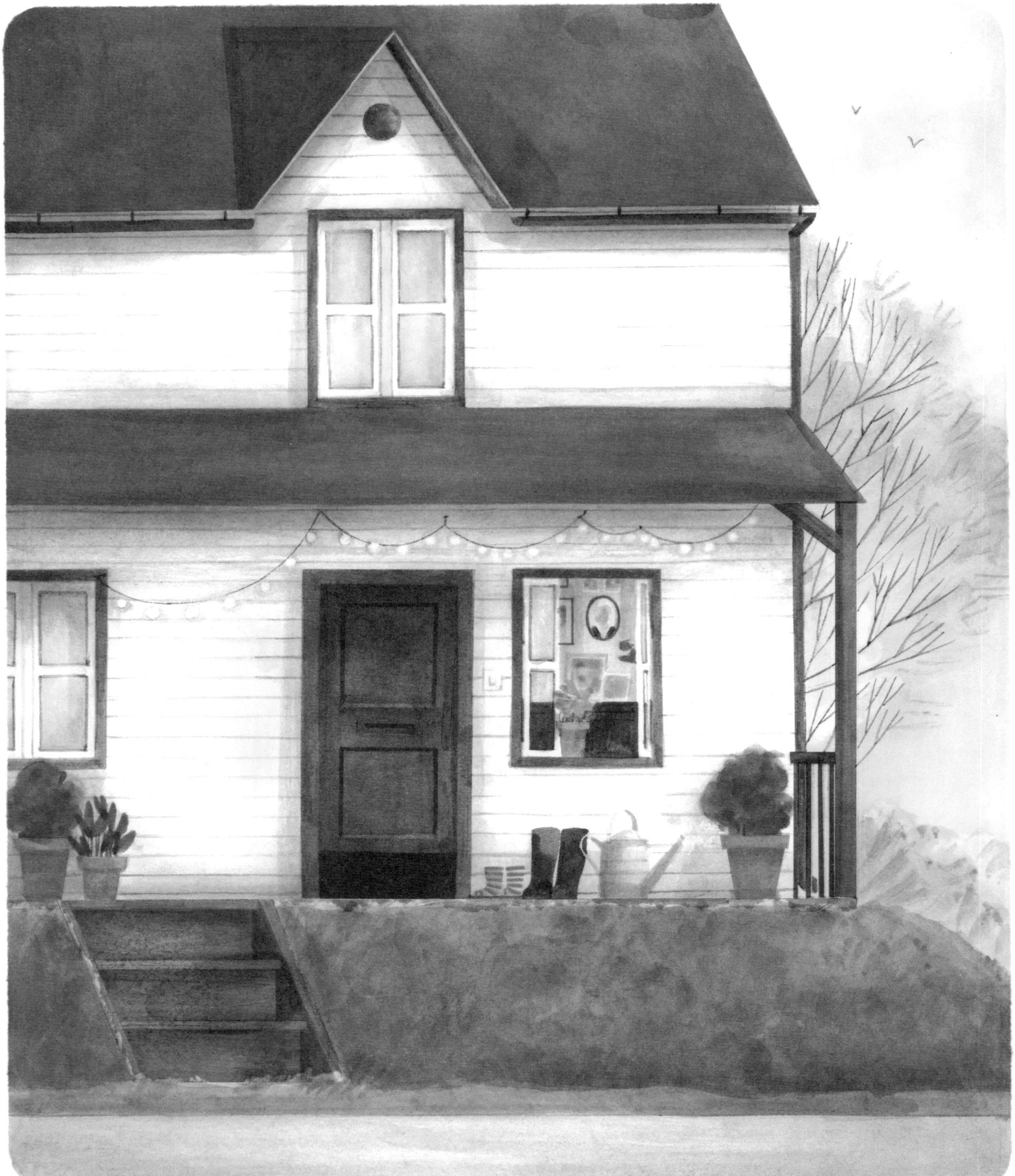

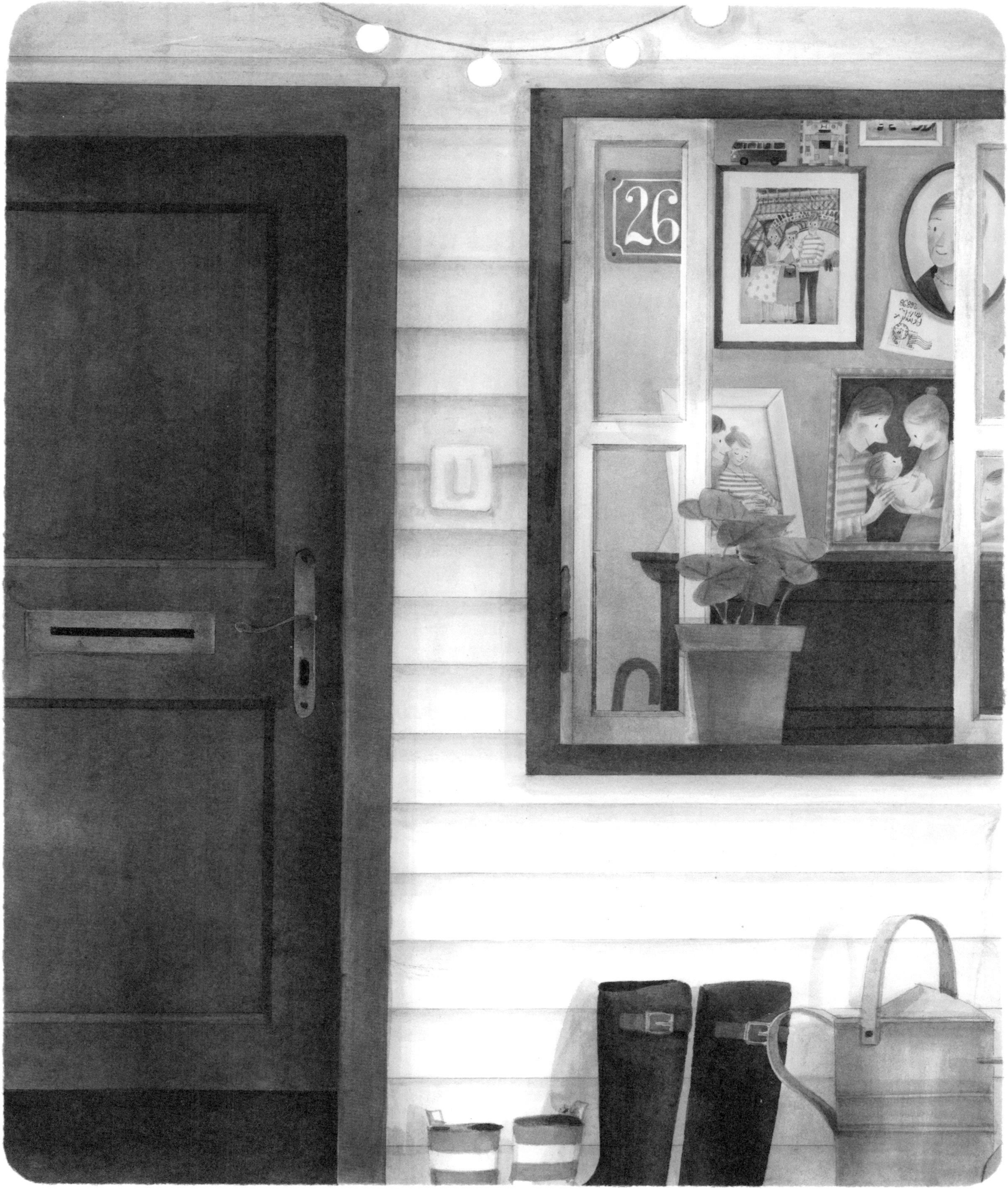
26

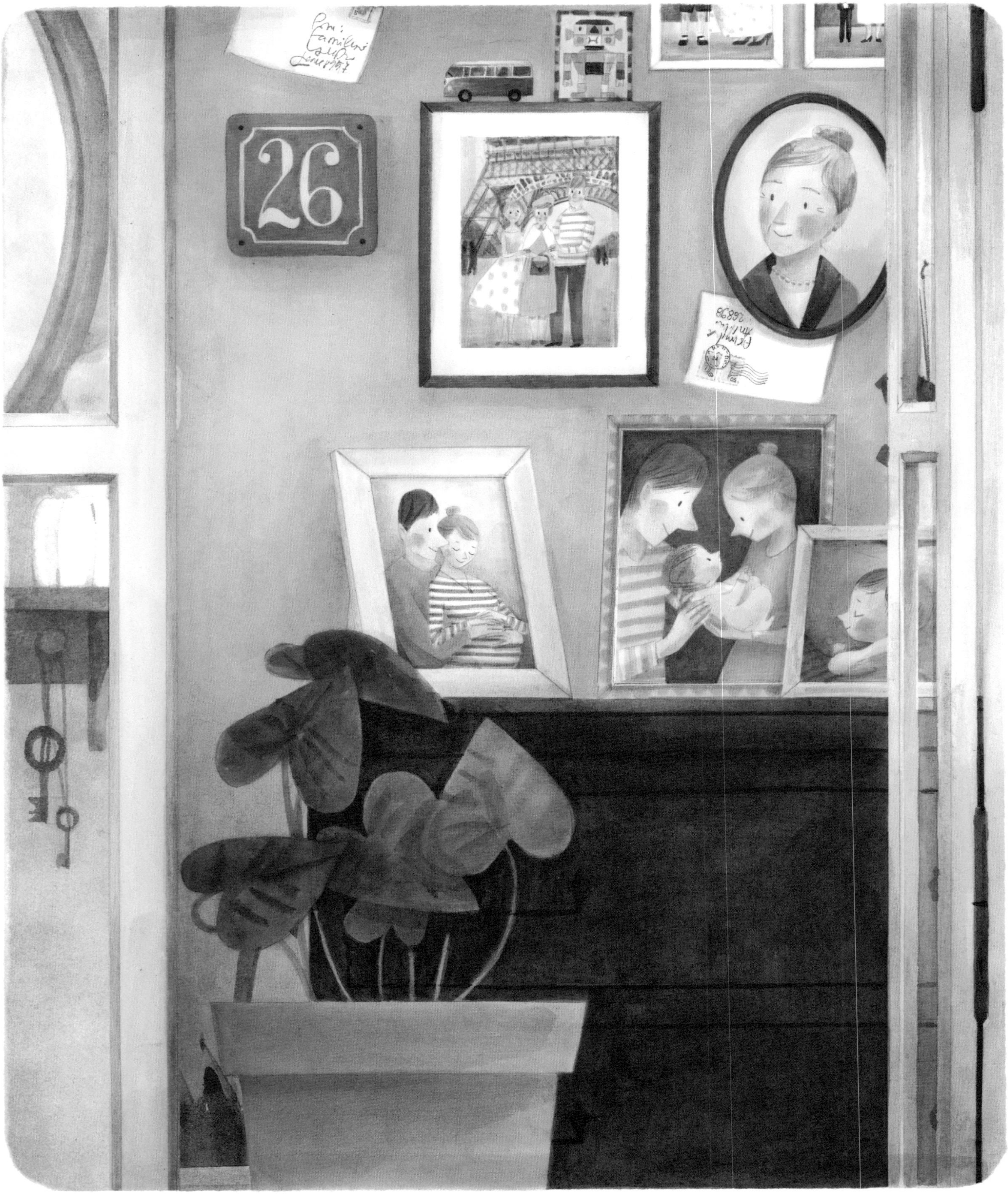
26

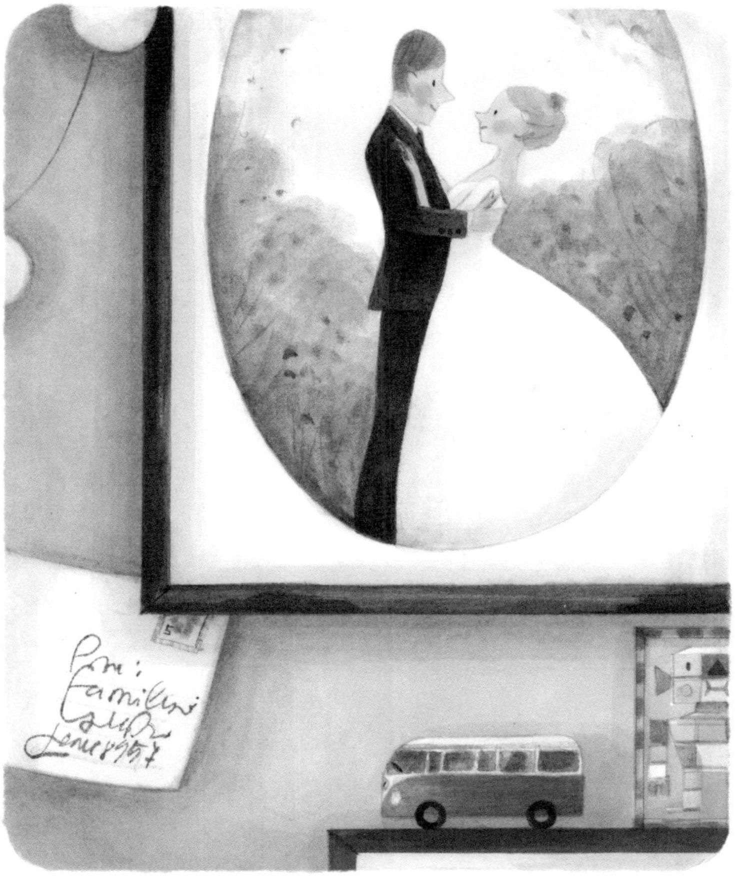

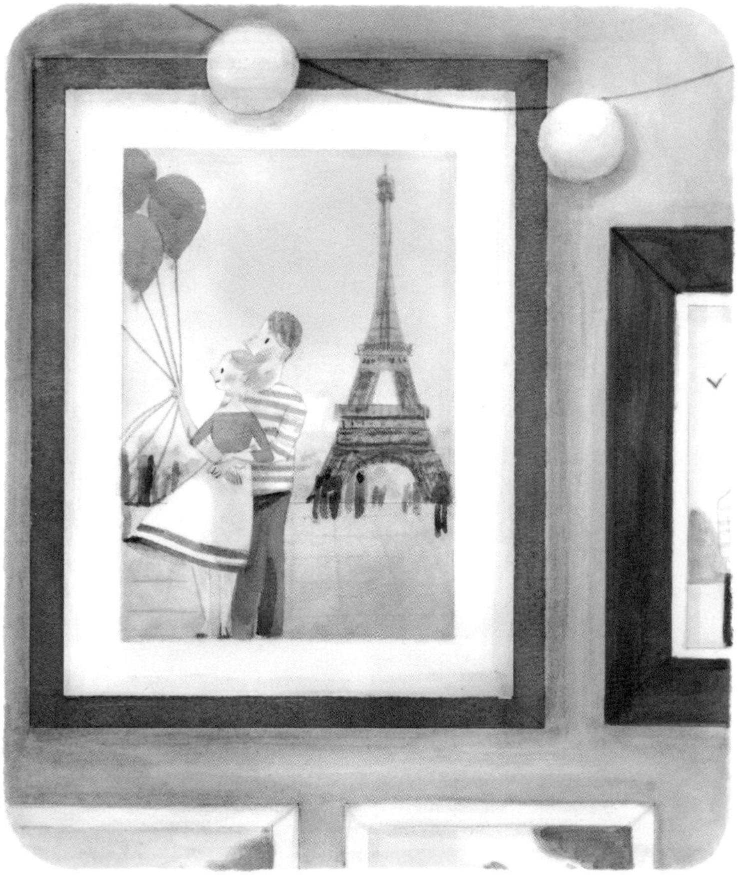

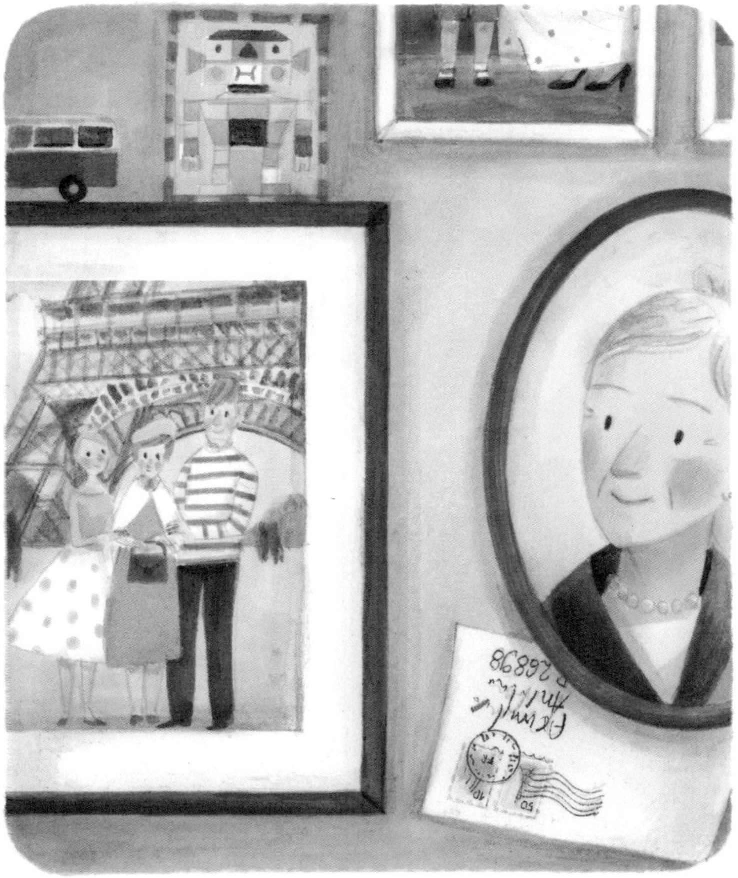

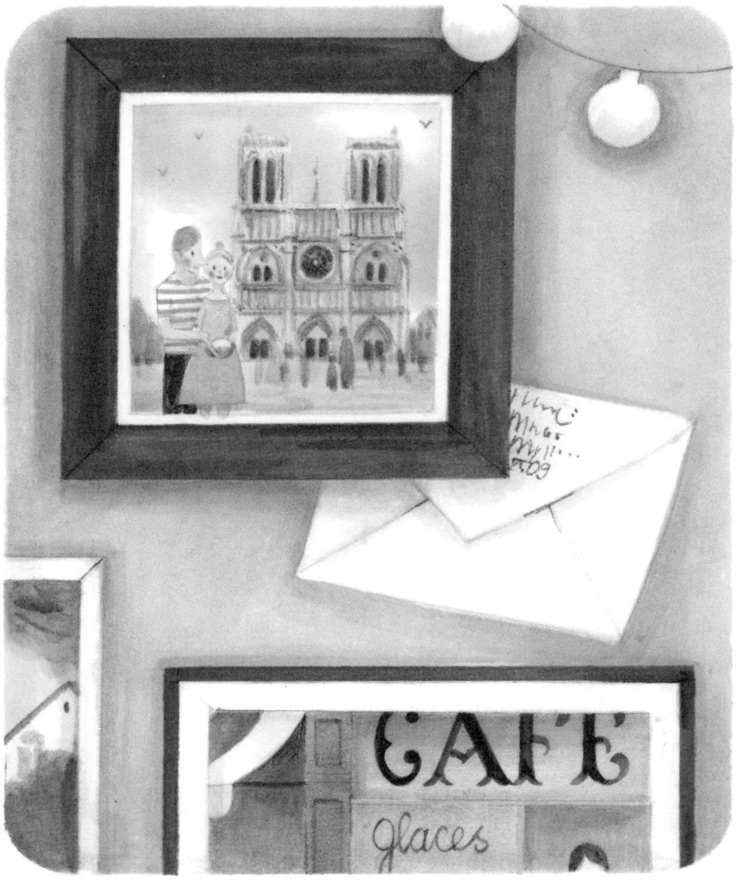
CAFE
glaces

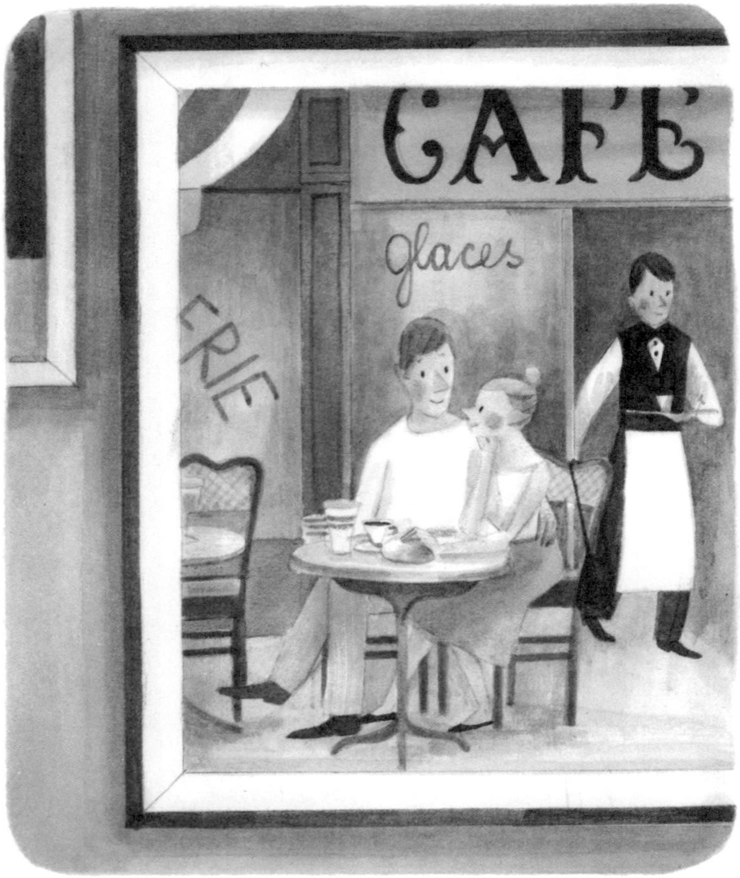
CAFÉ
glaces
ERIE

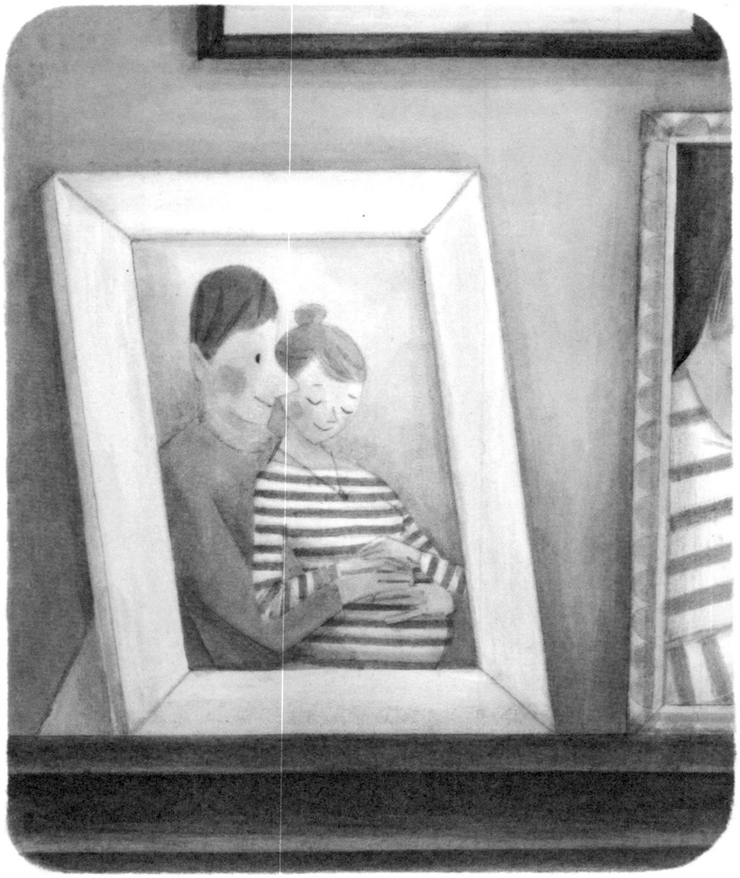

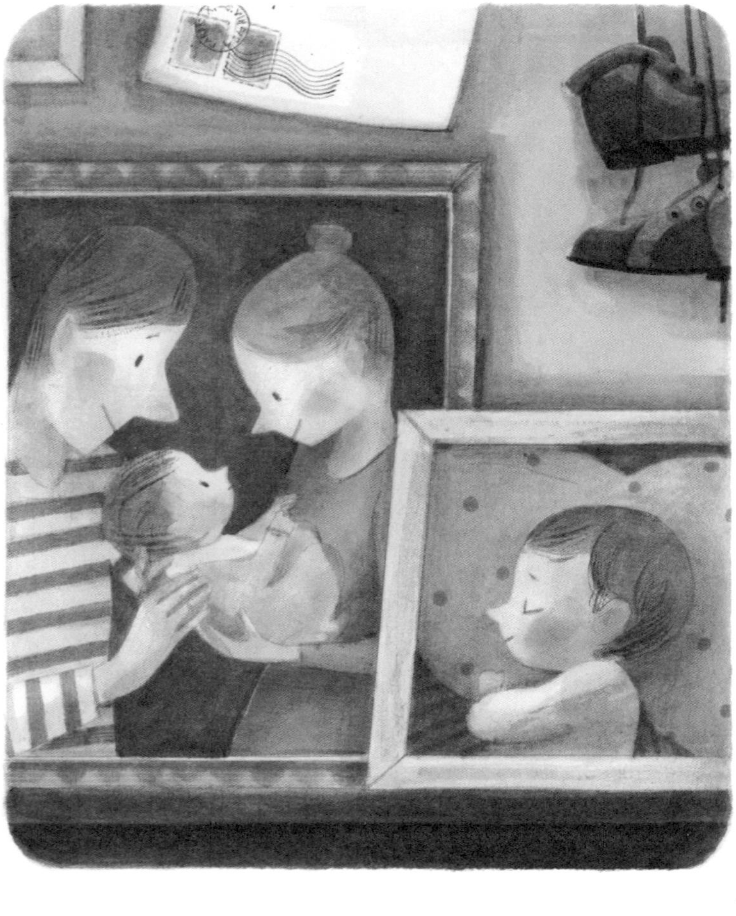

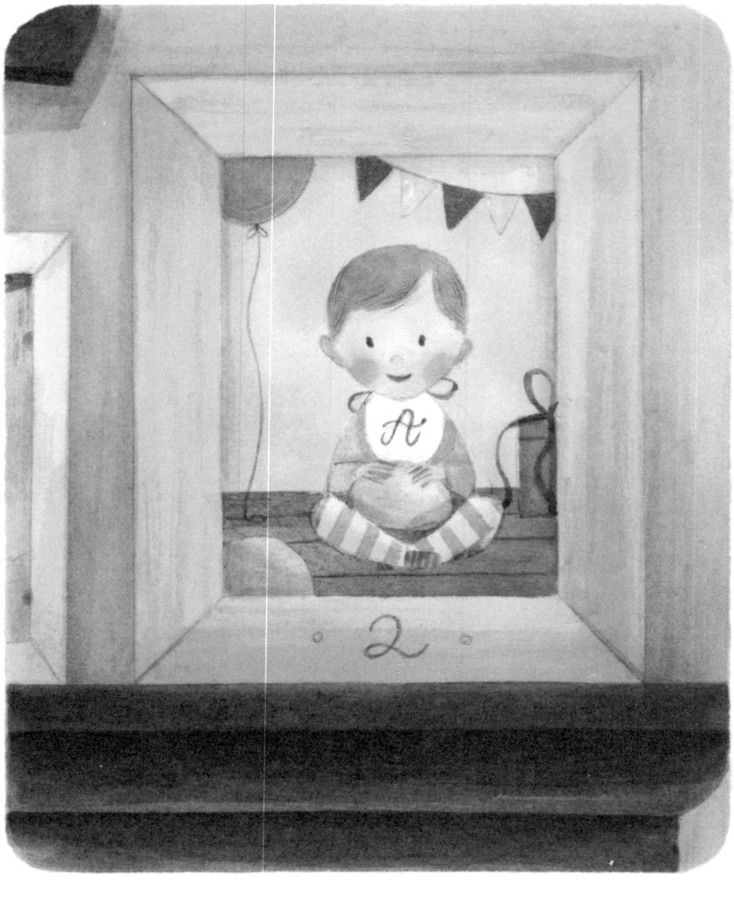
A
2

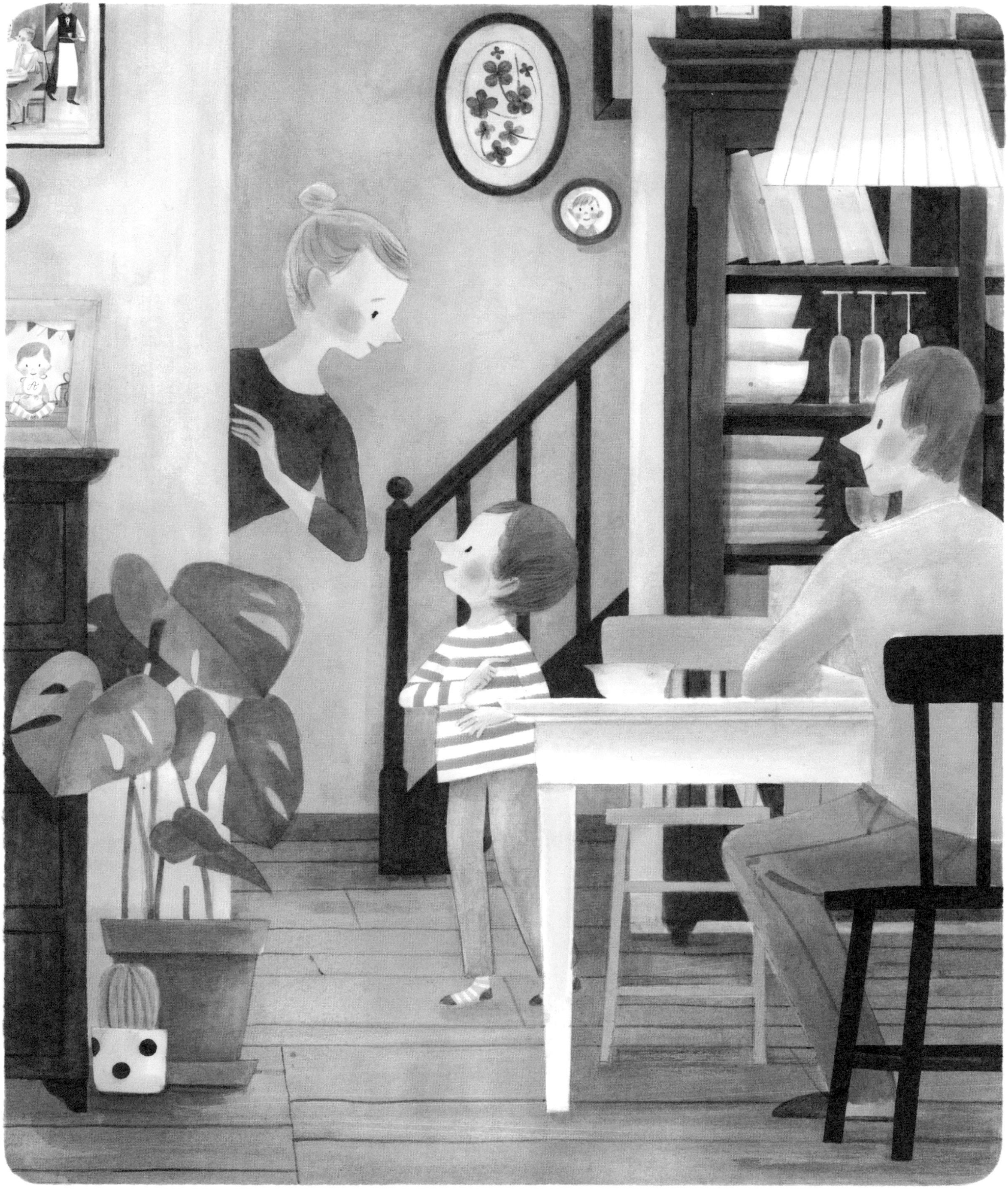

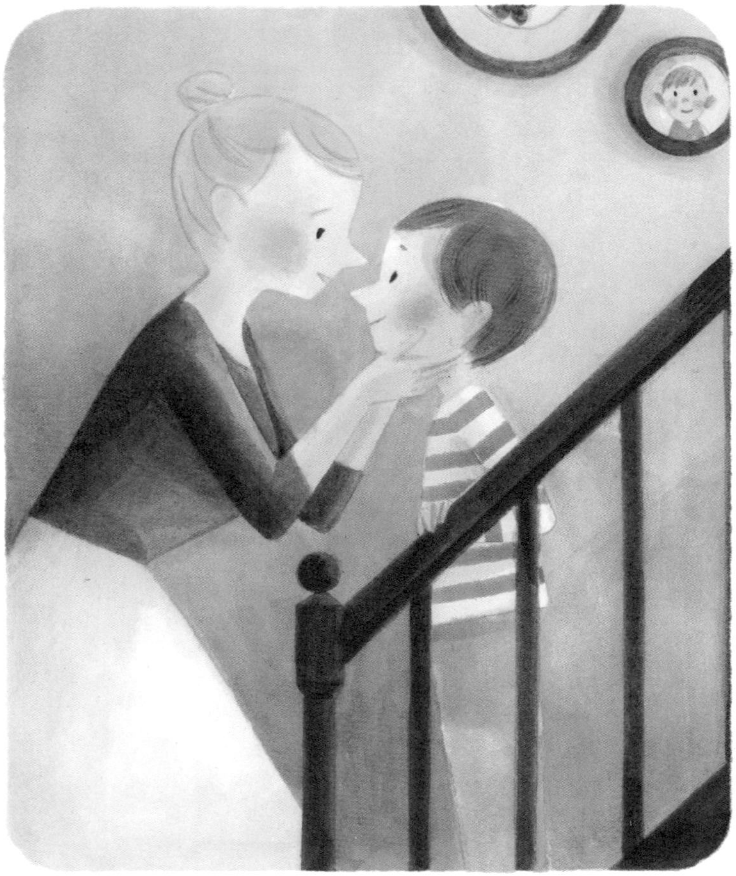

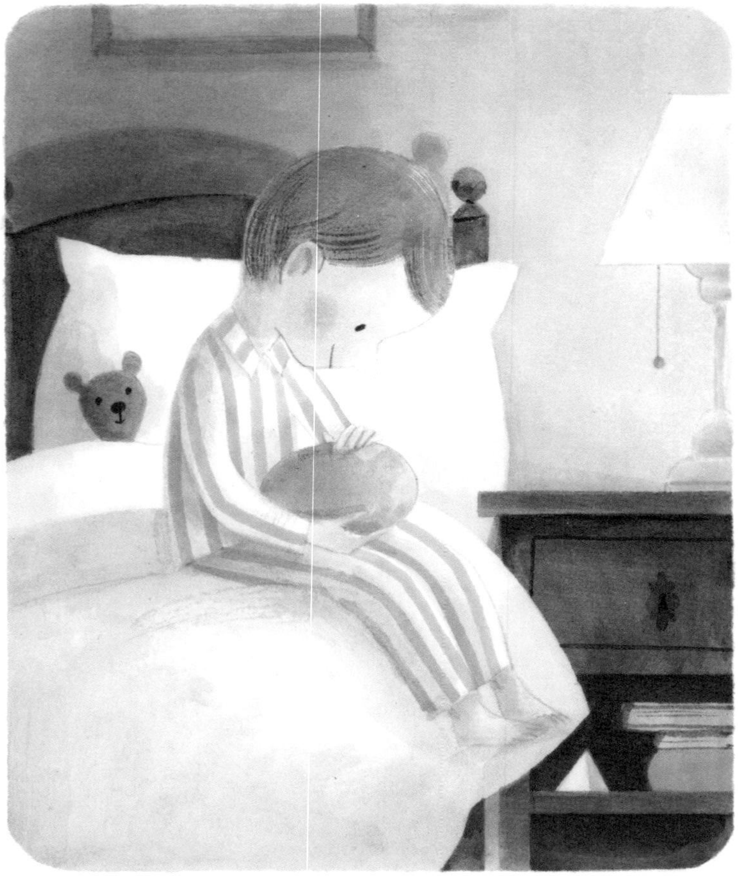

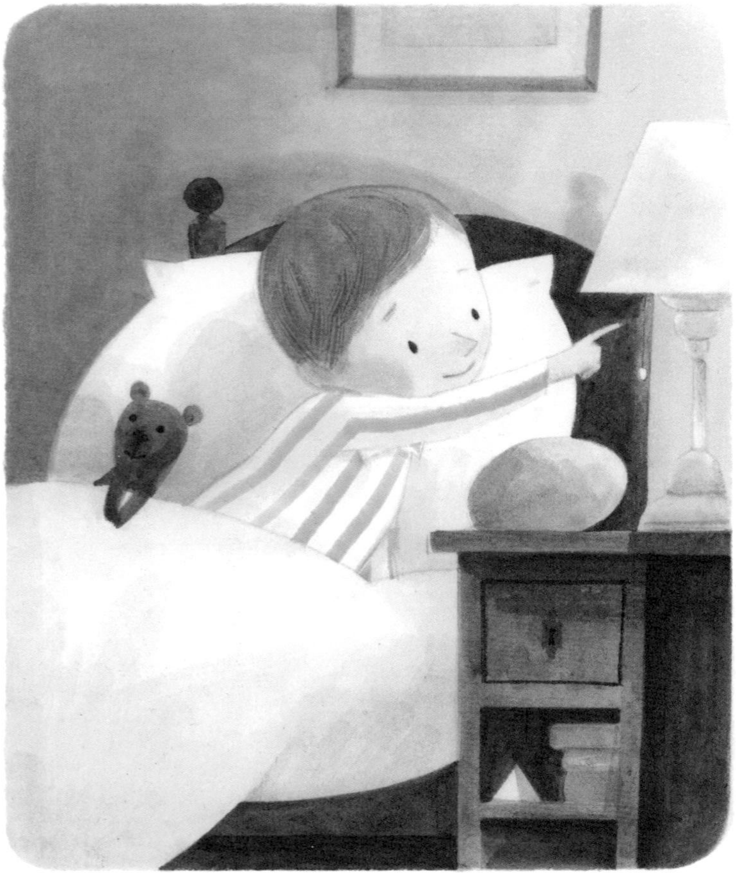

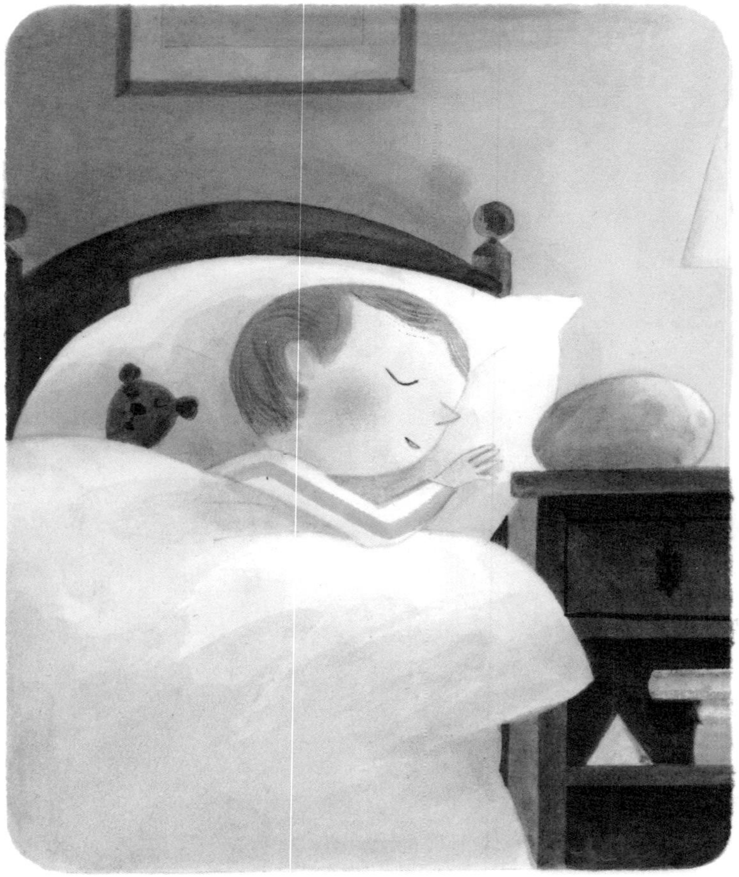

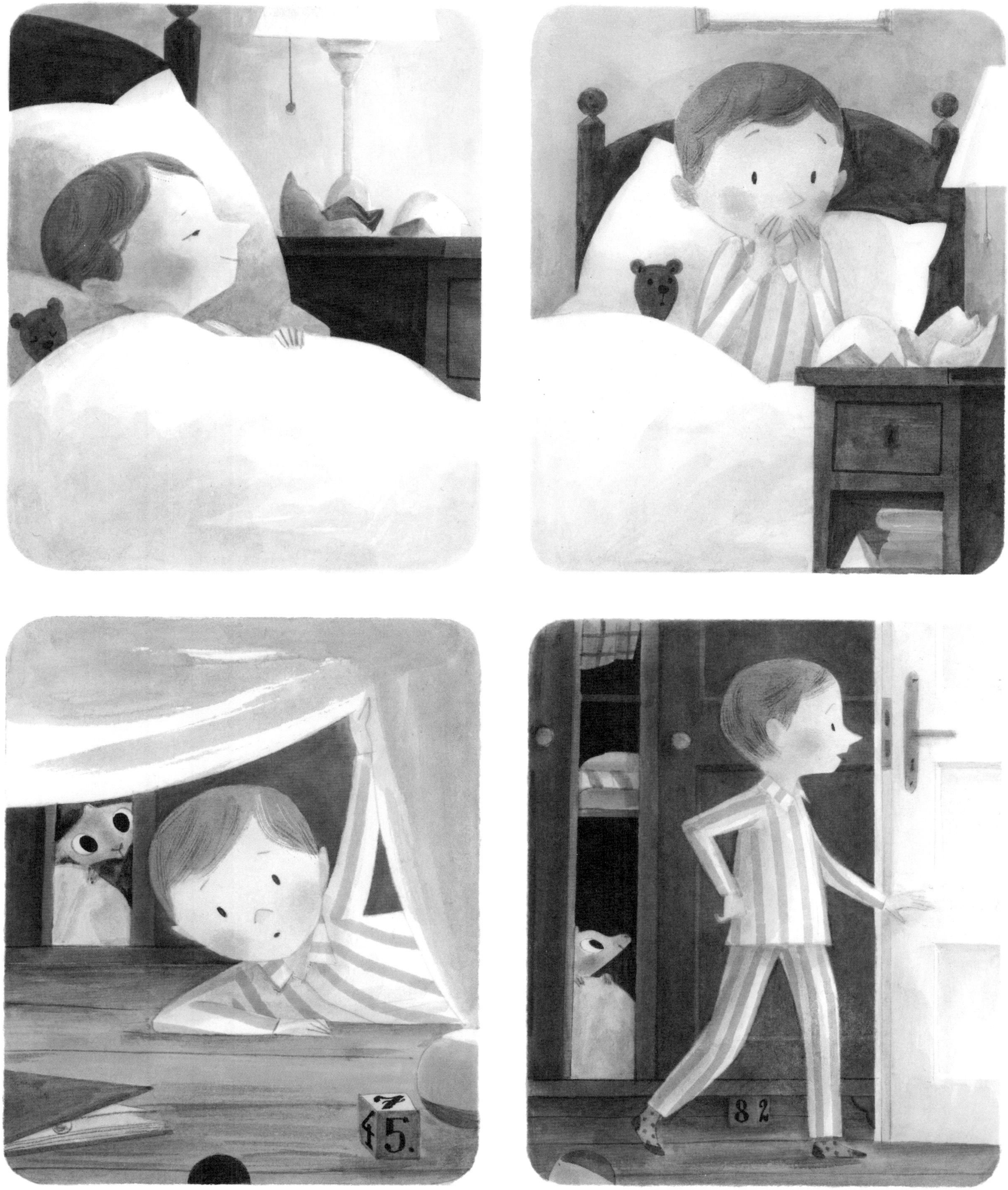

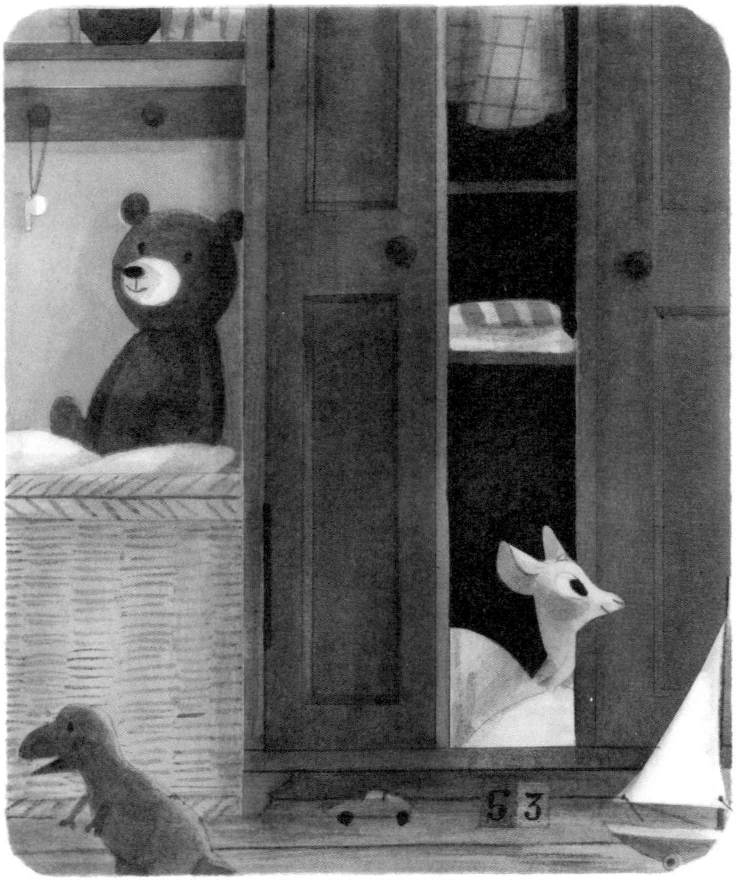
5 3

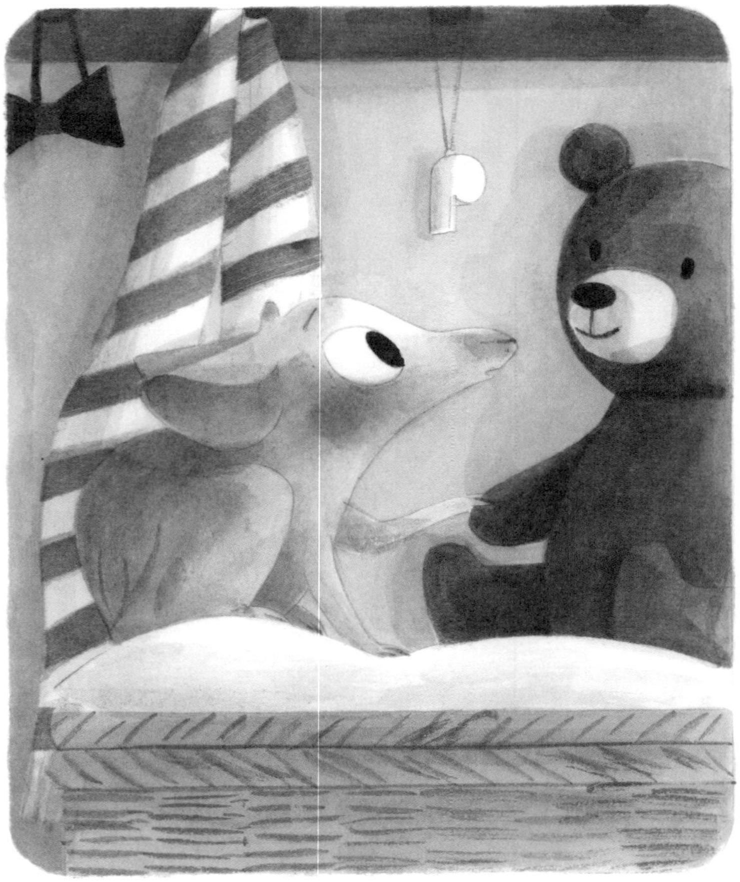

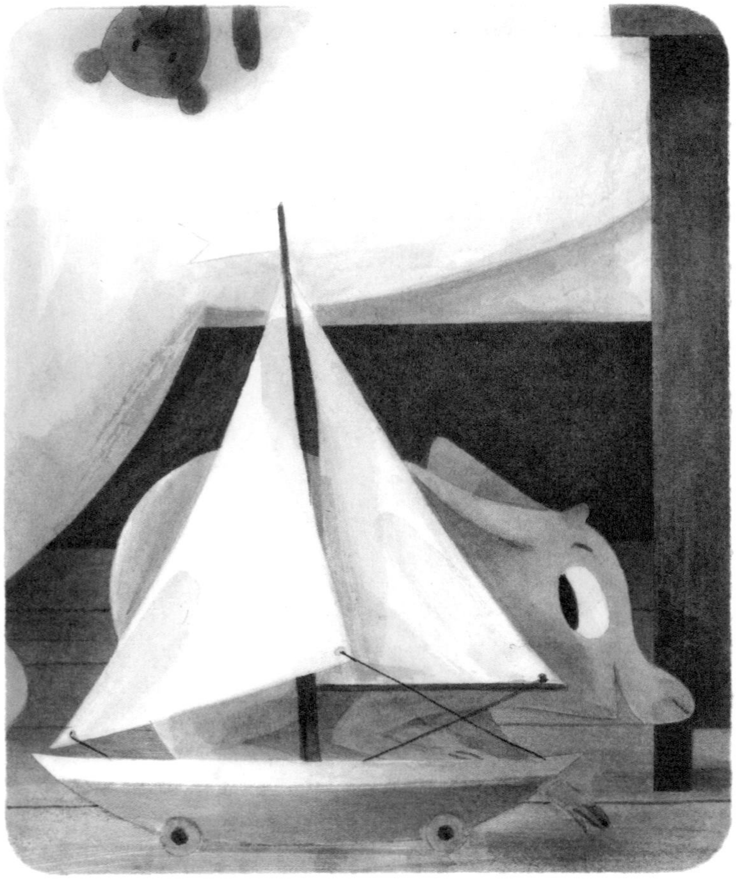

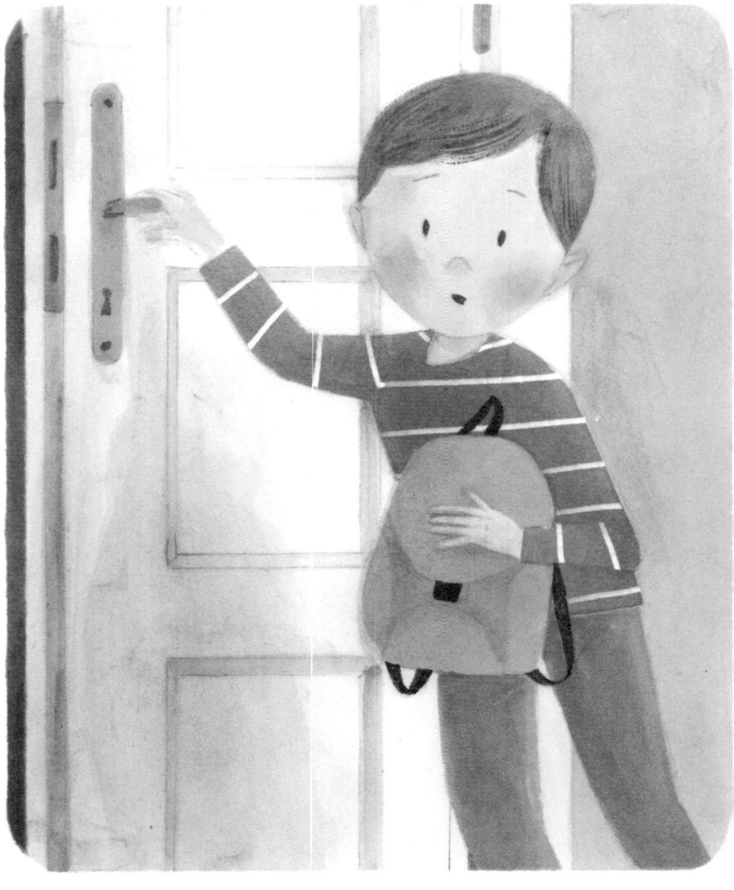

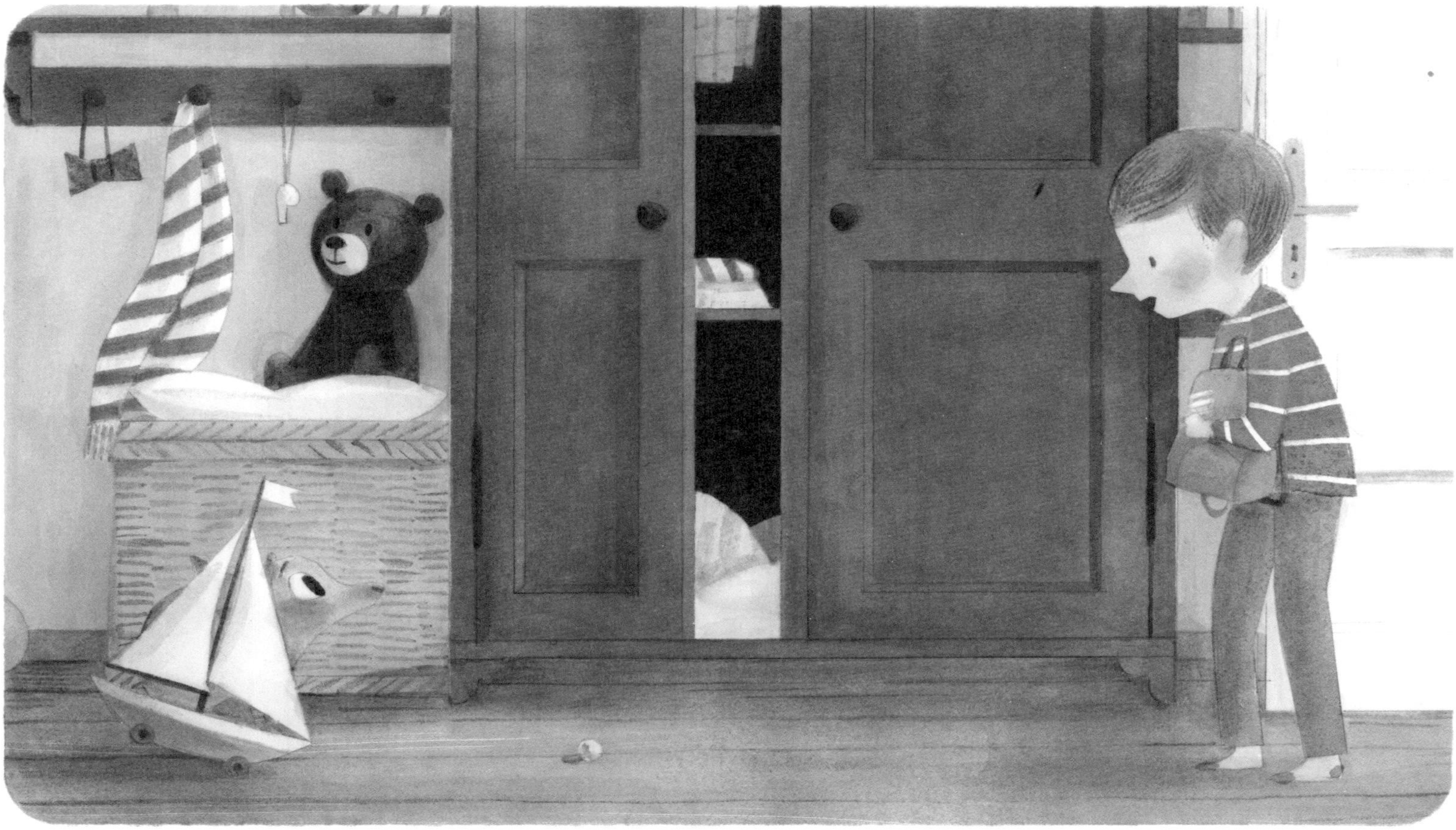

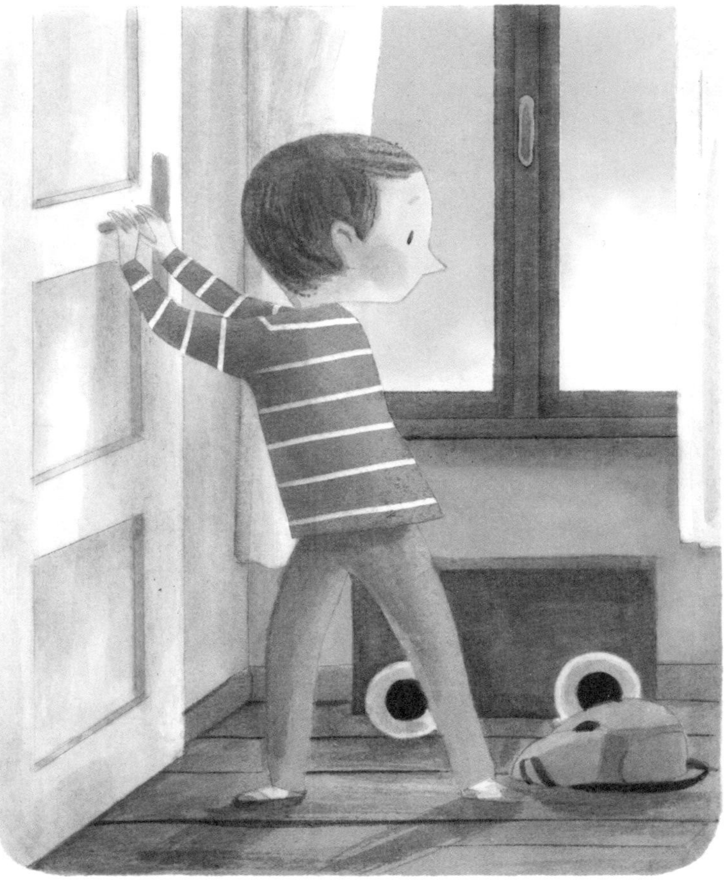

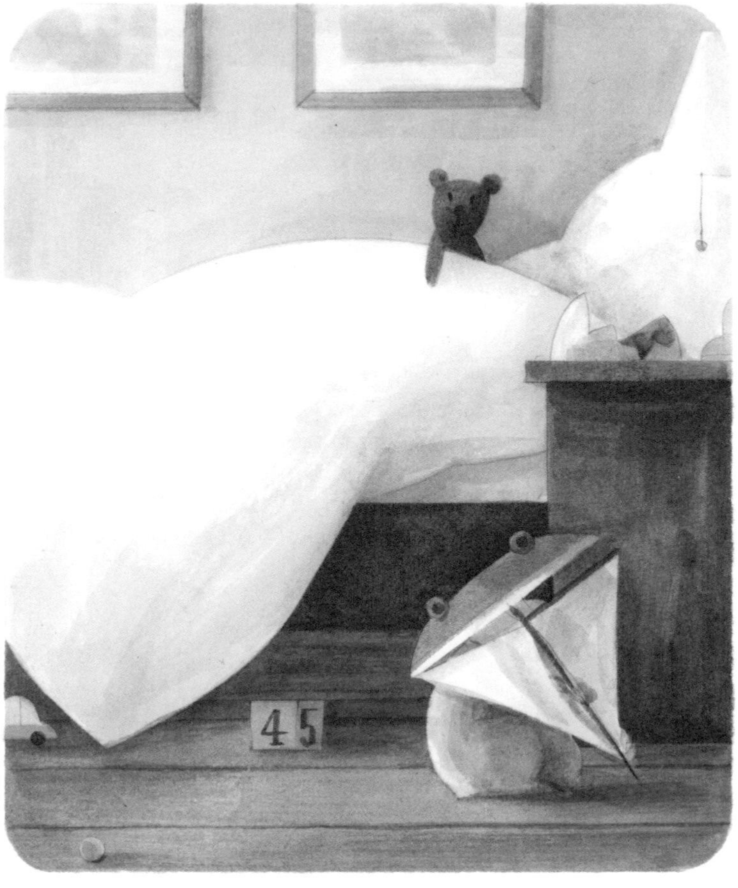
45

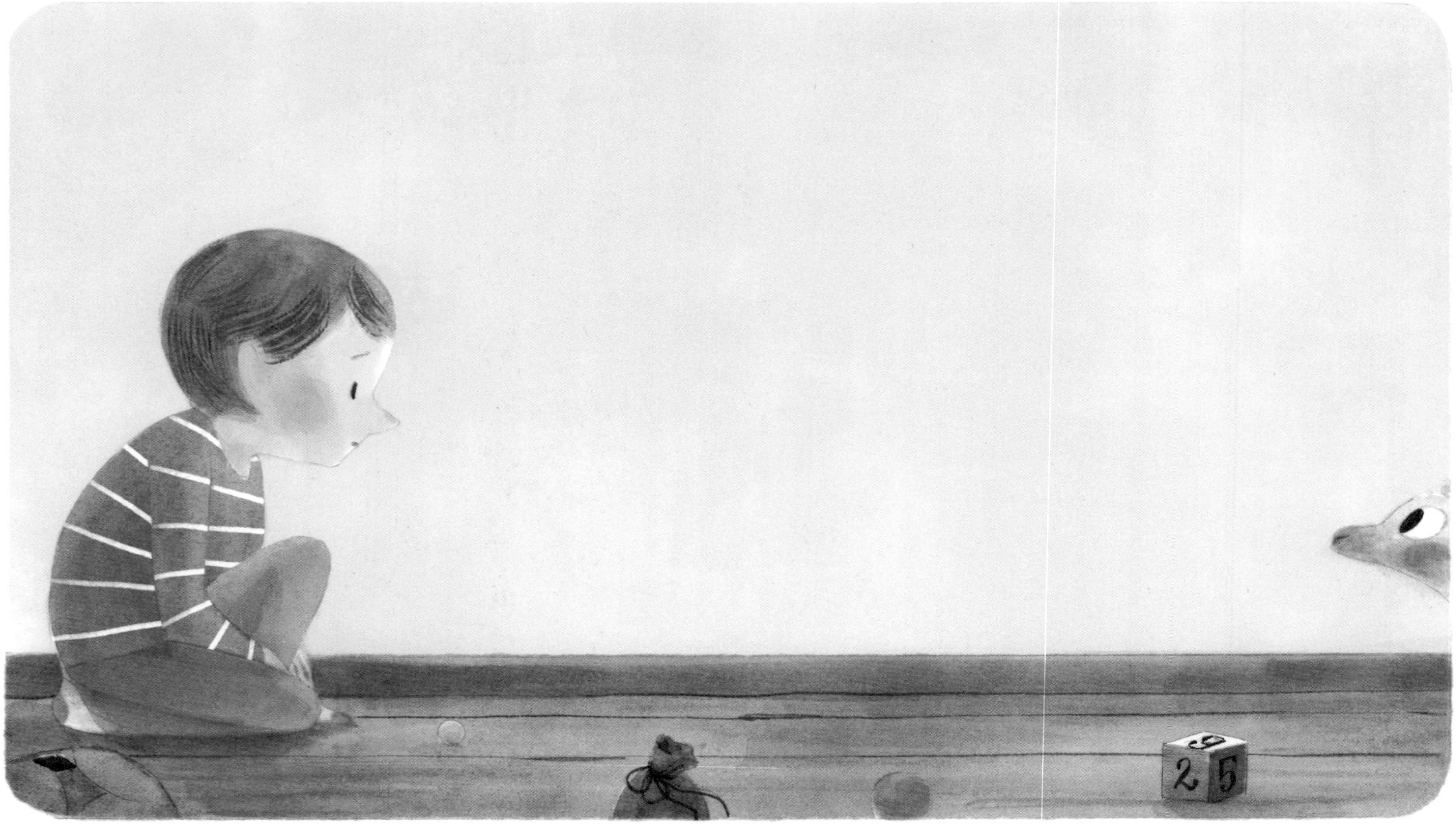
2 5

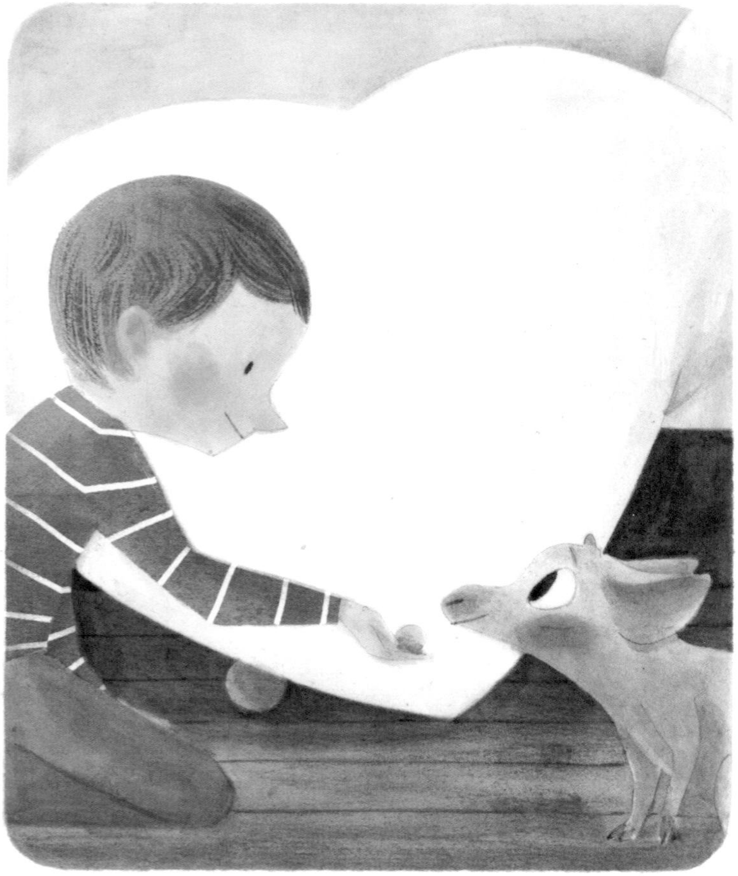

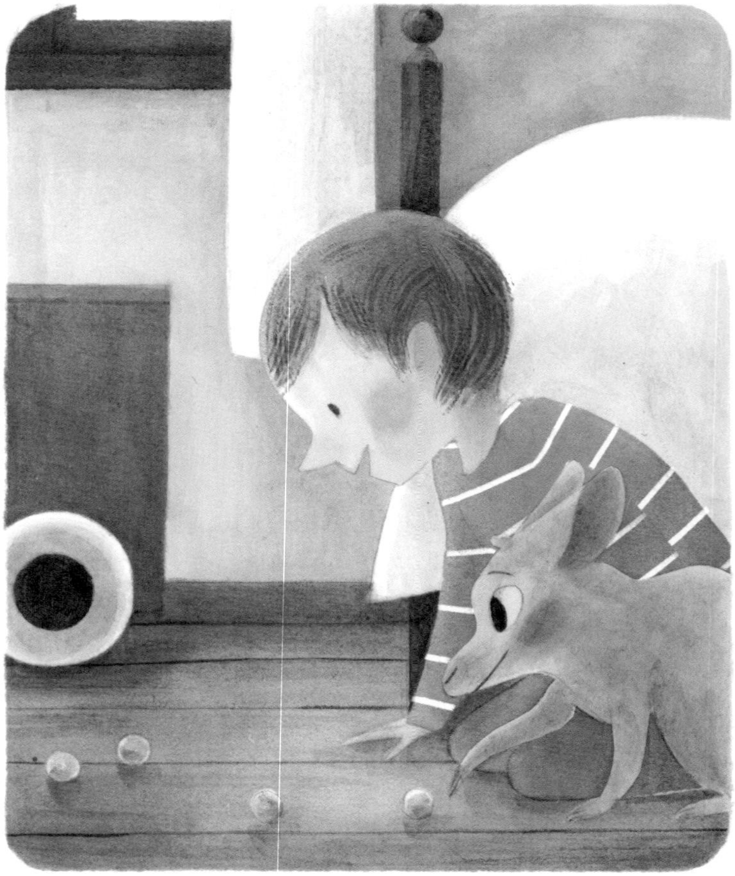

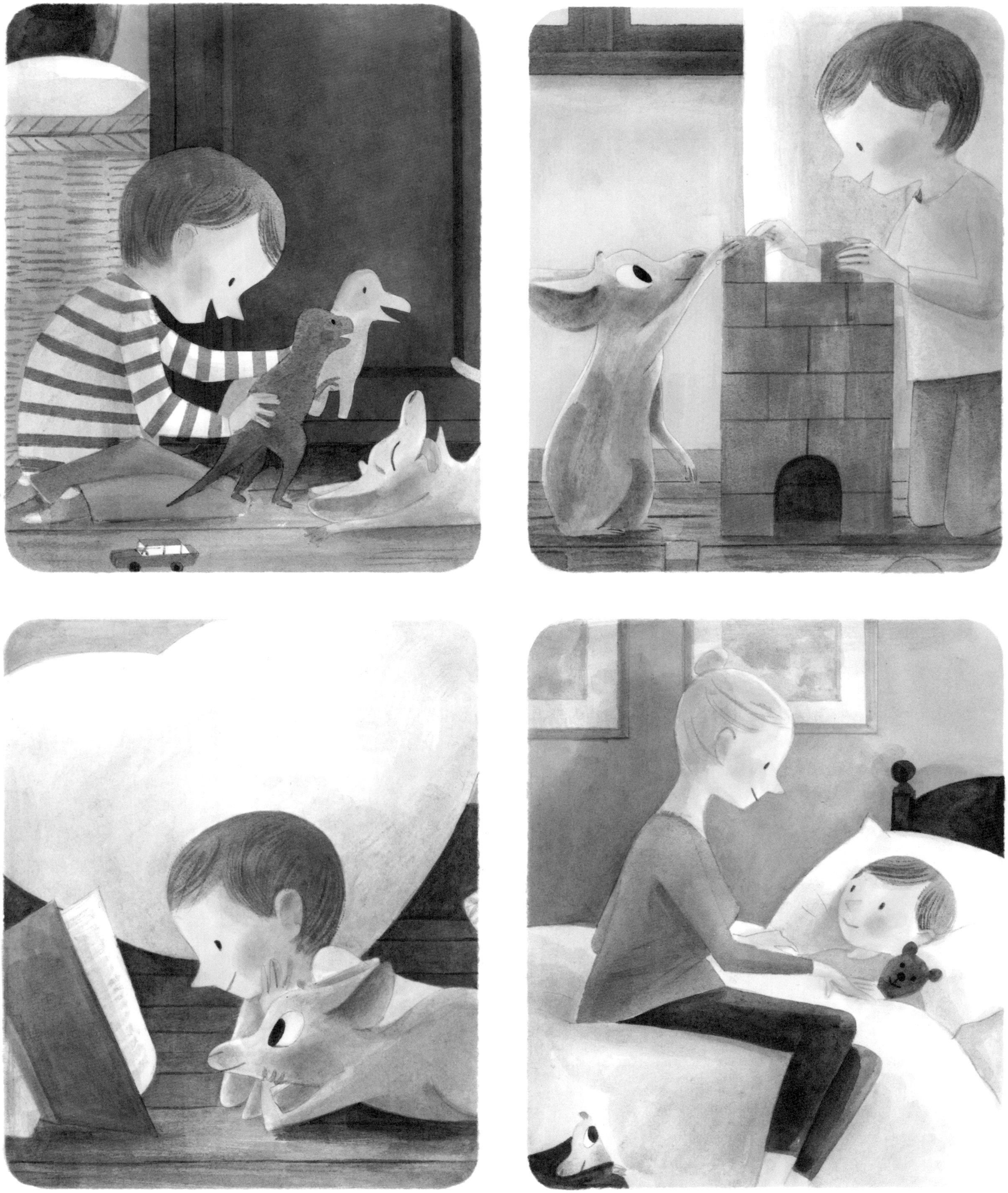

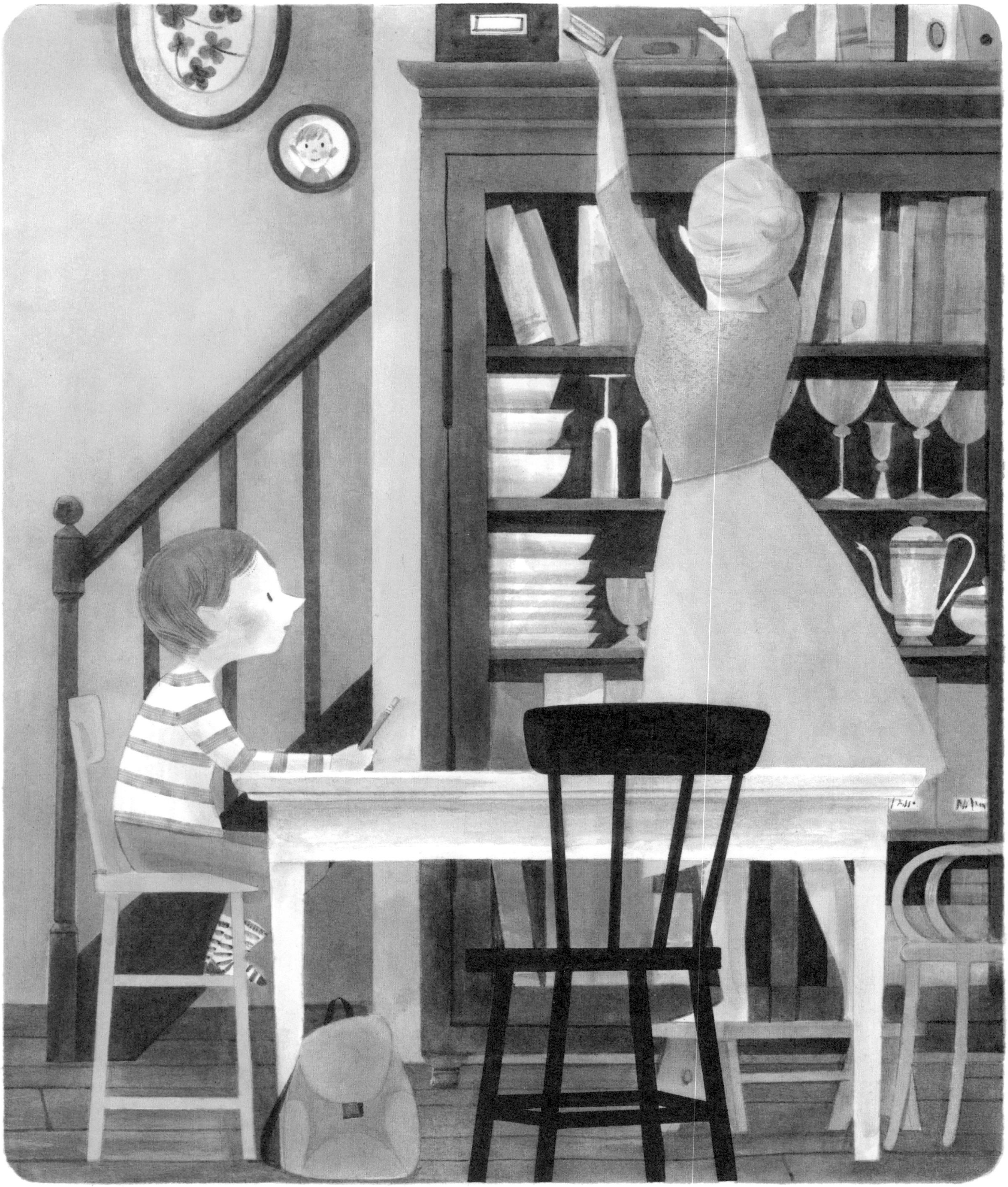

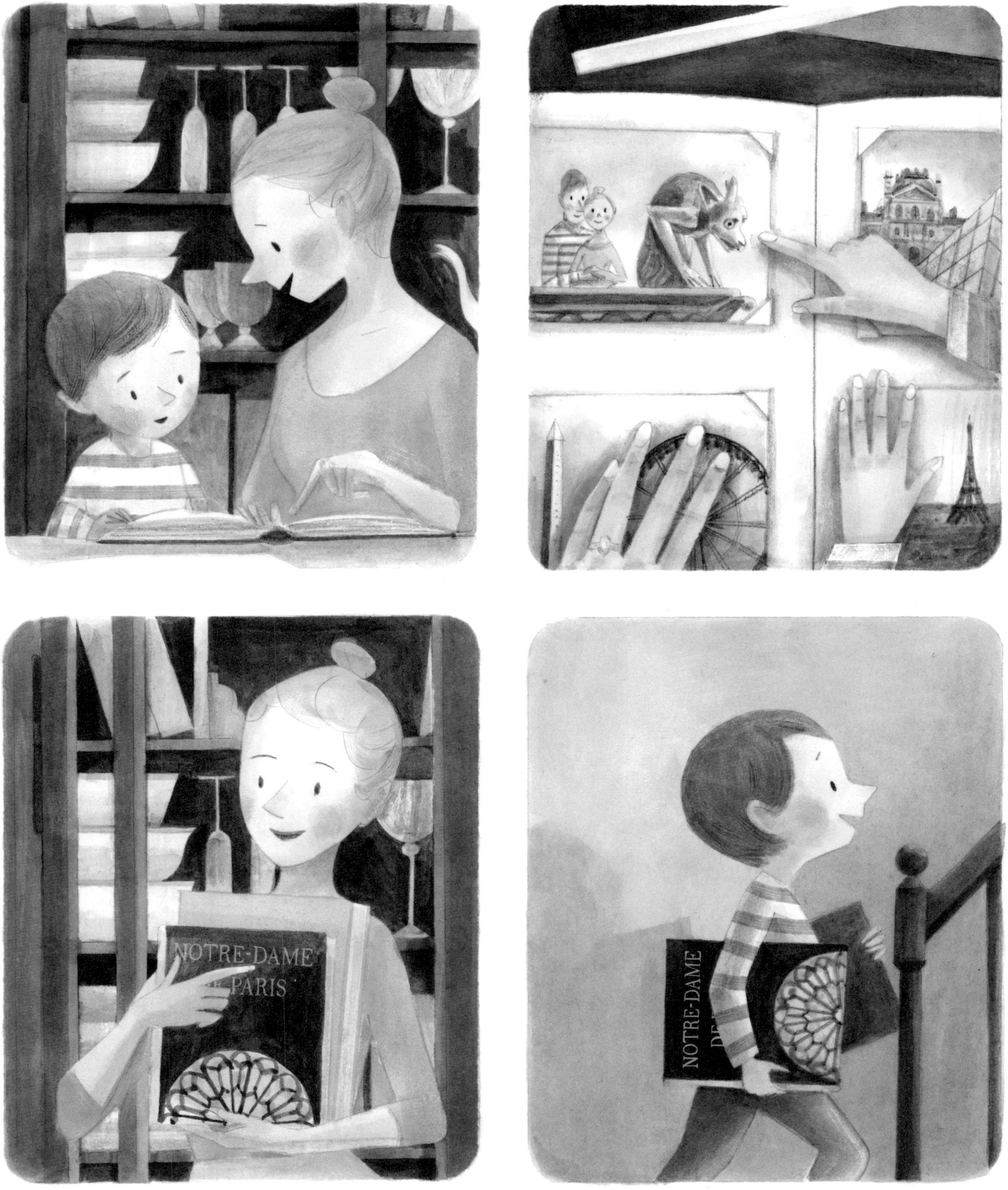
NOTRE-DAME
PARIS
NOTRE-DAME
DE

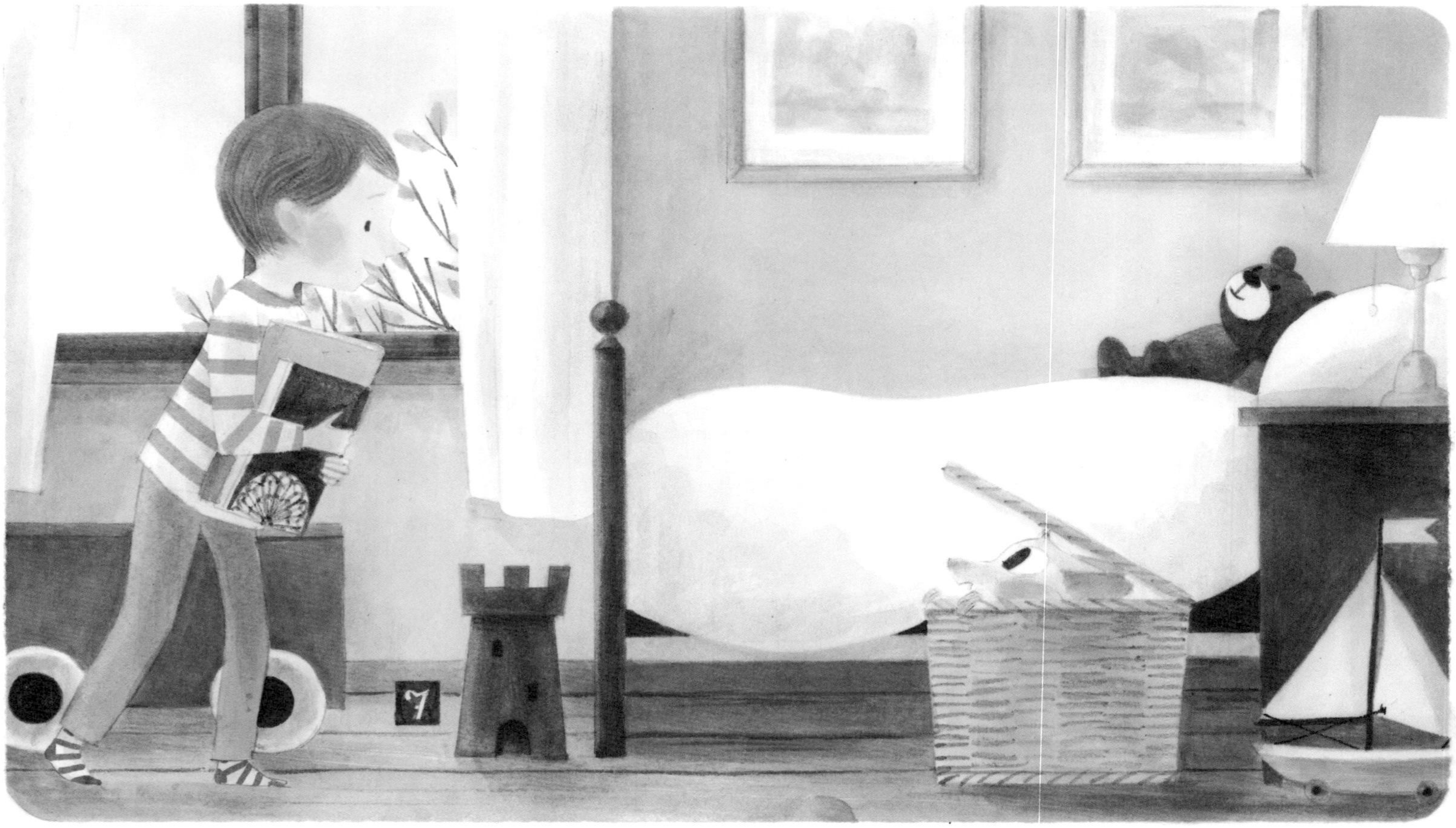
7

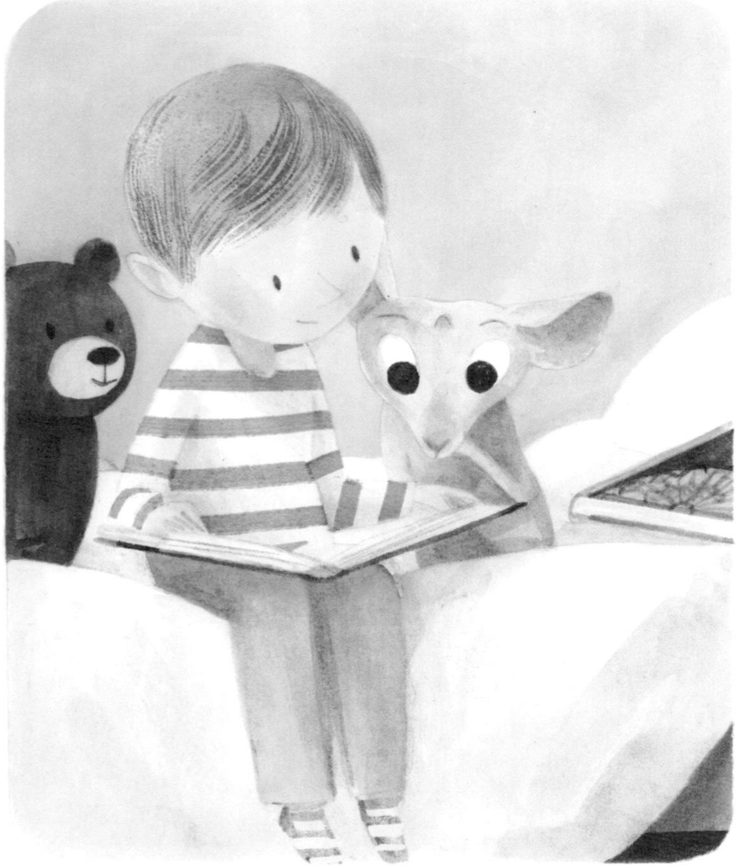

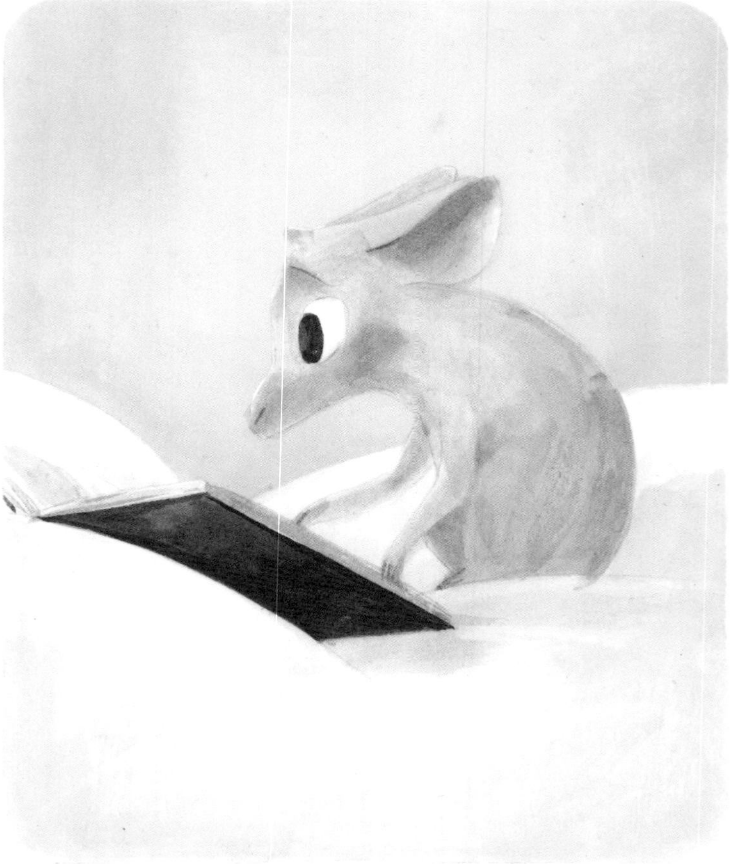

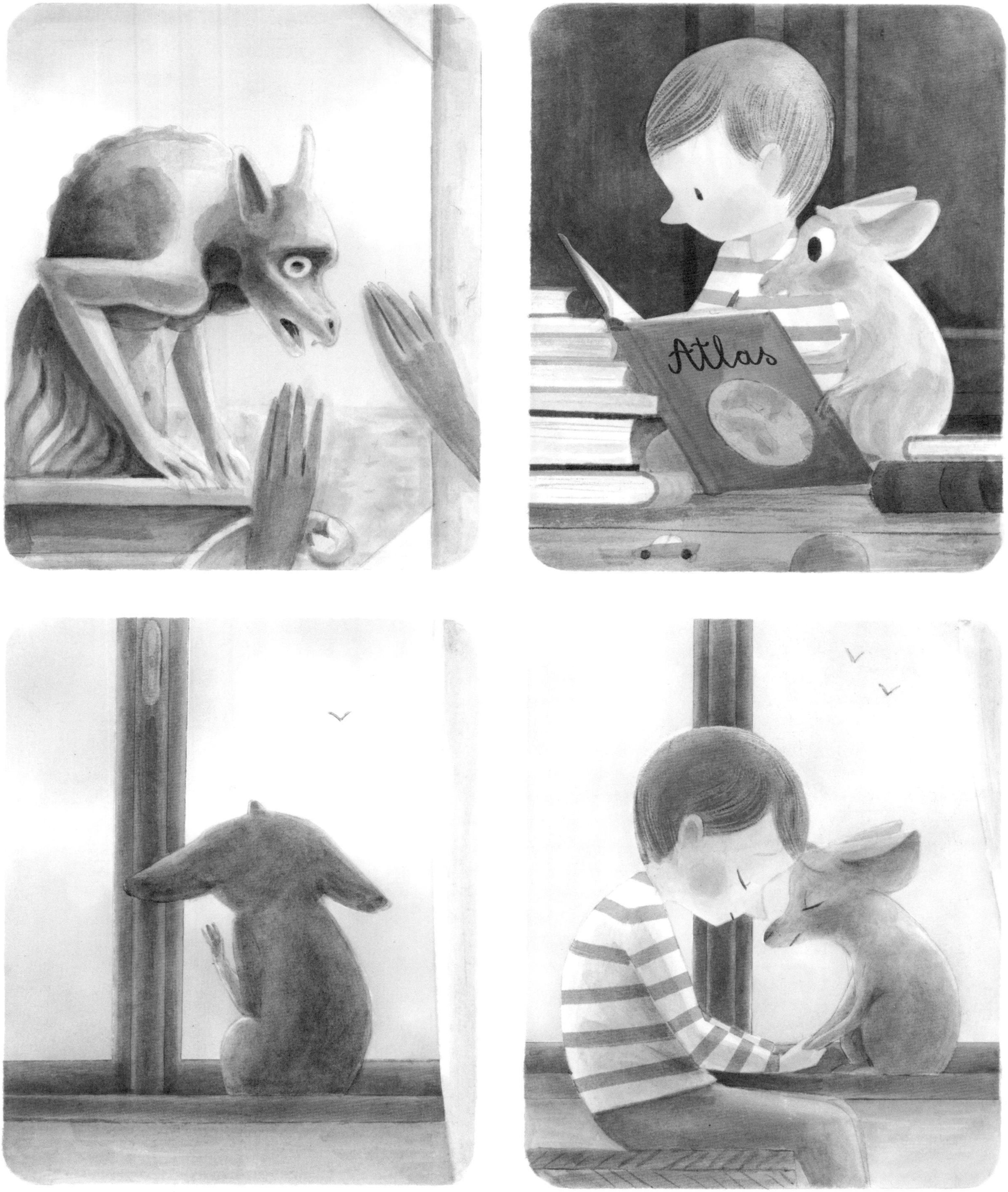
Atlas

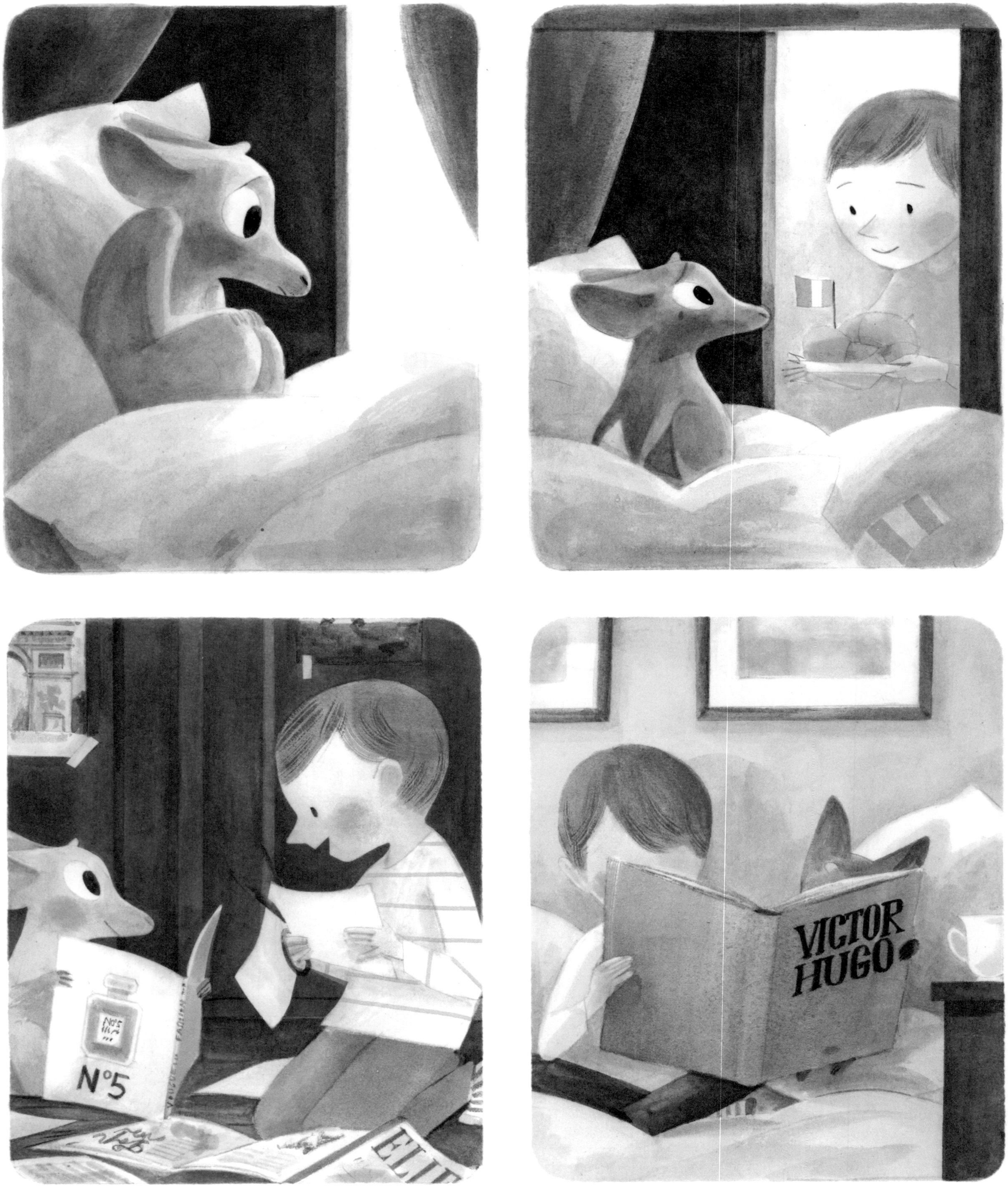
N°5
VICTOR
HUGO

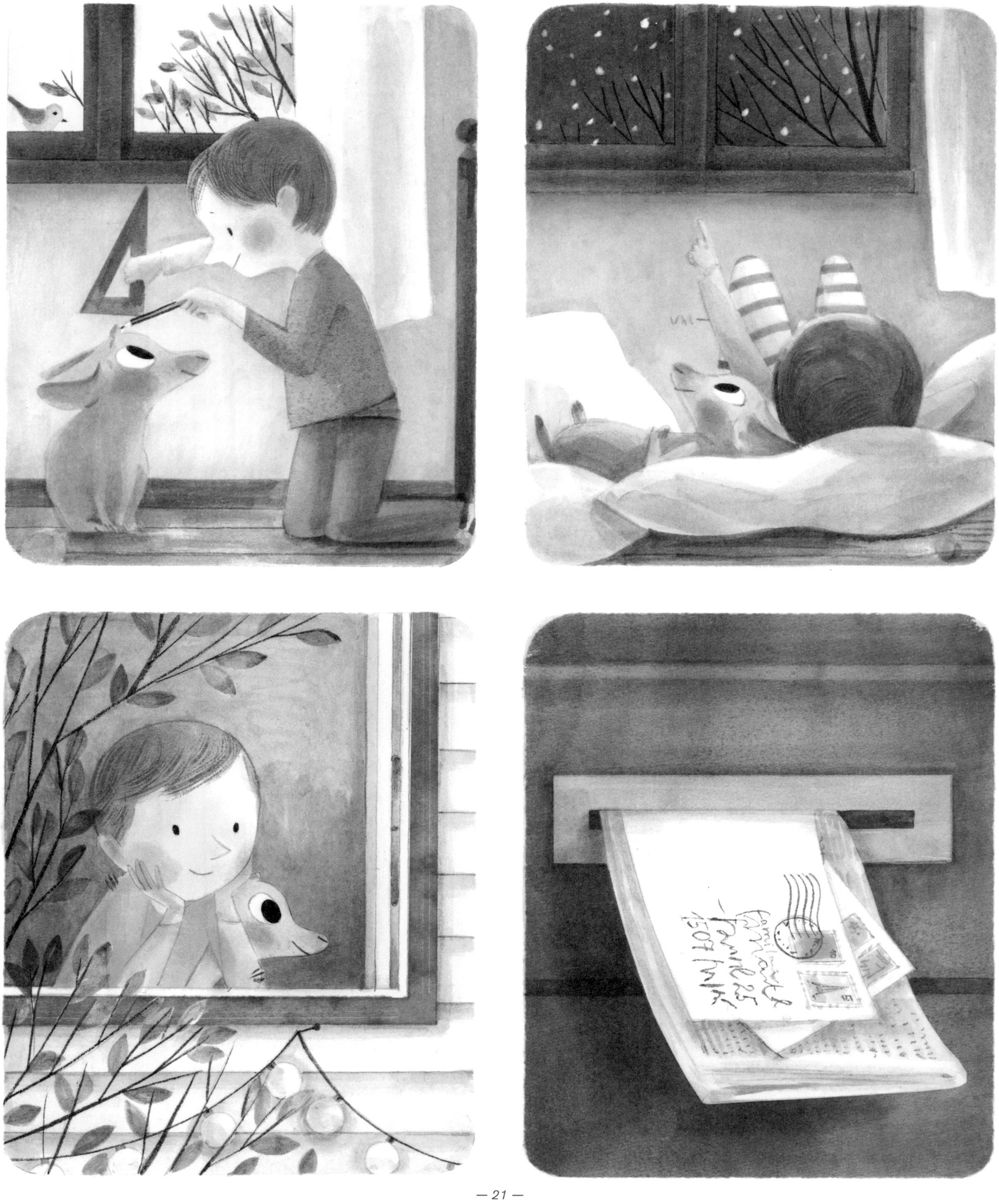

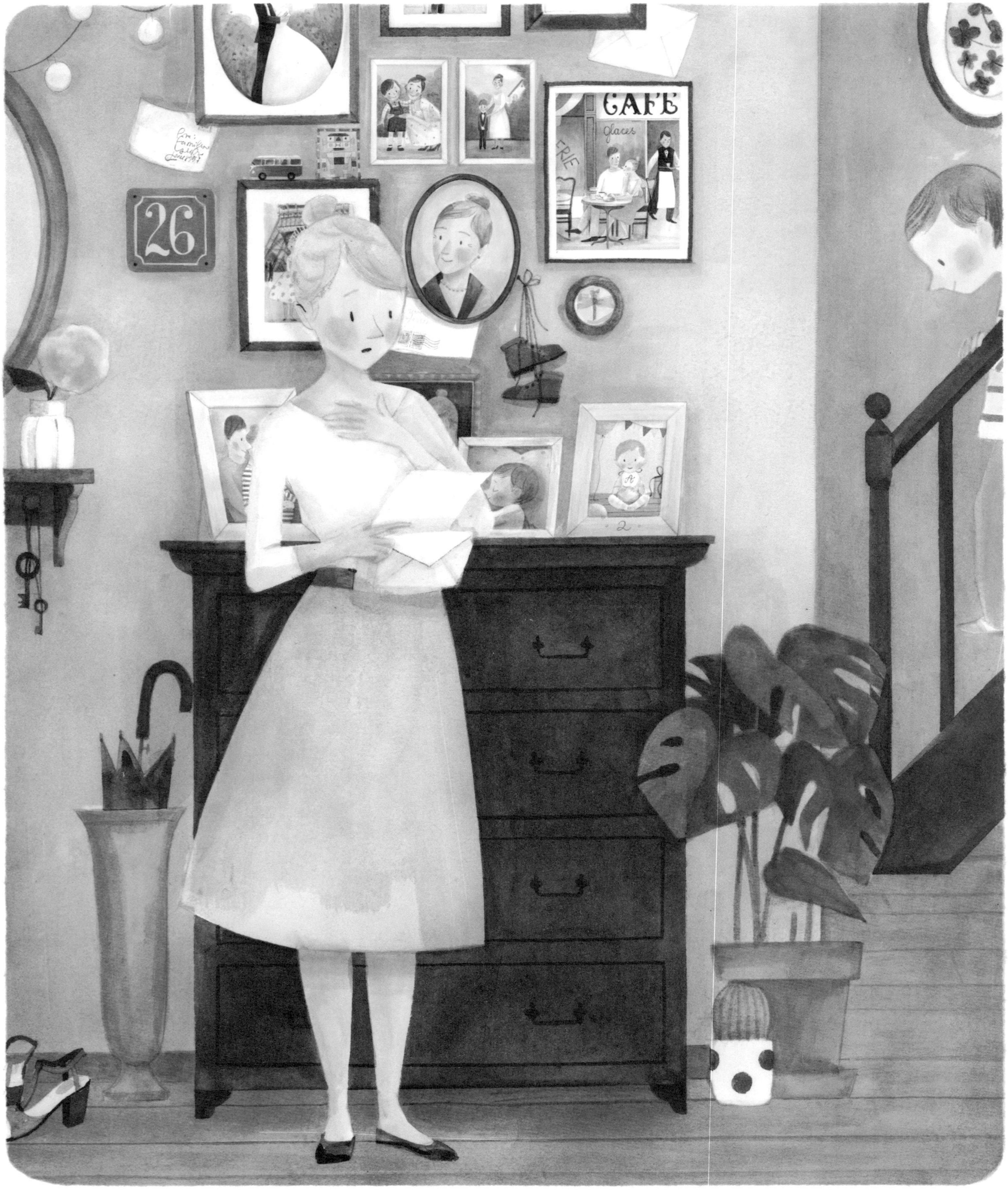
26
CAFE
glaces

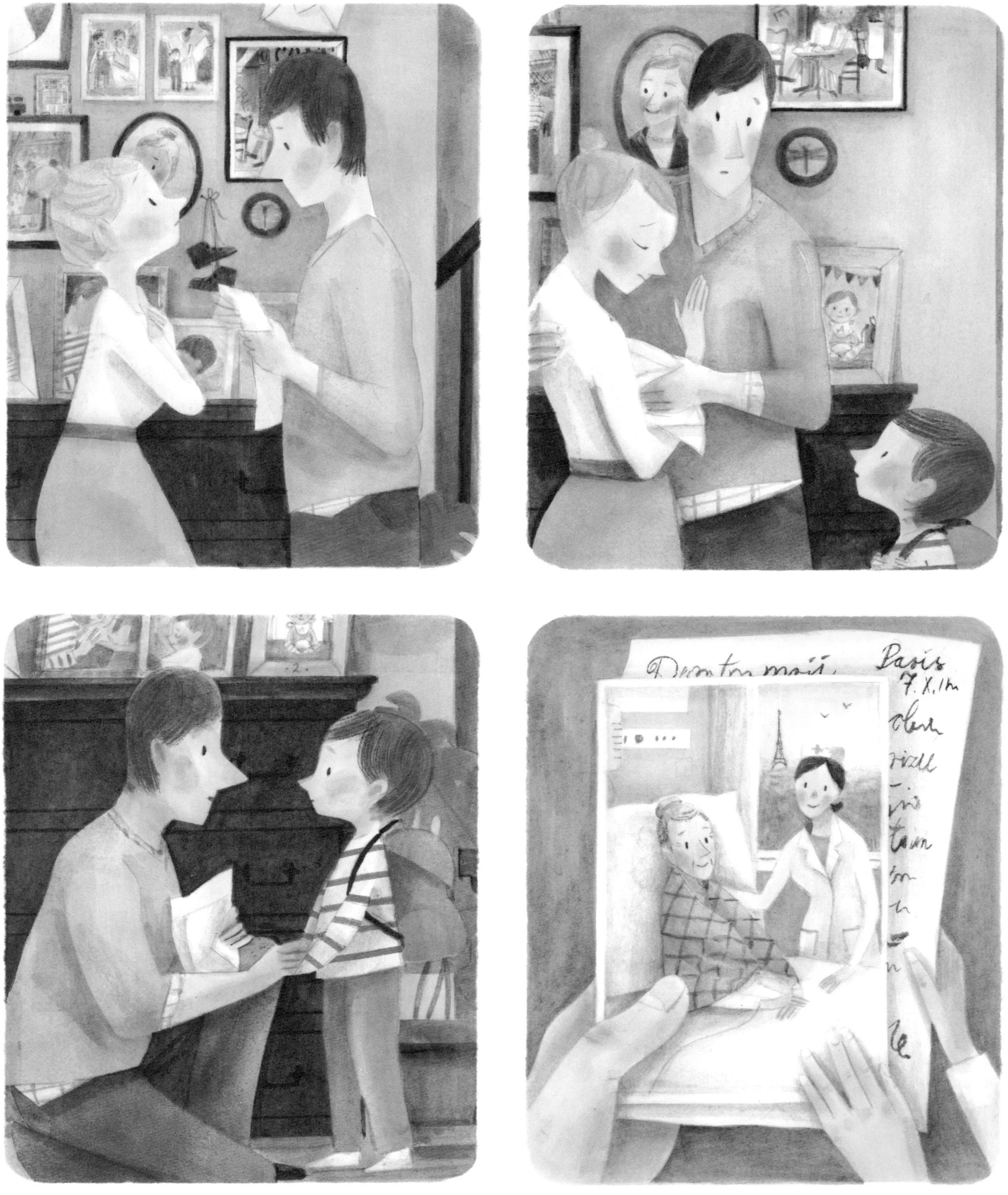
Paris

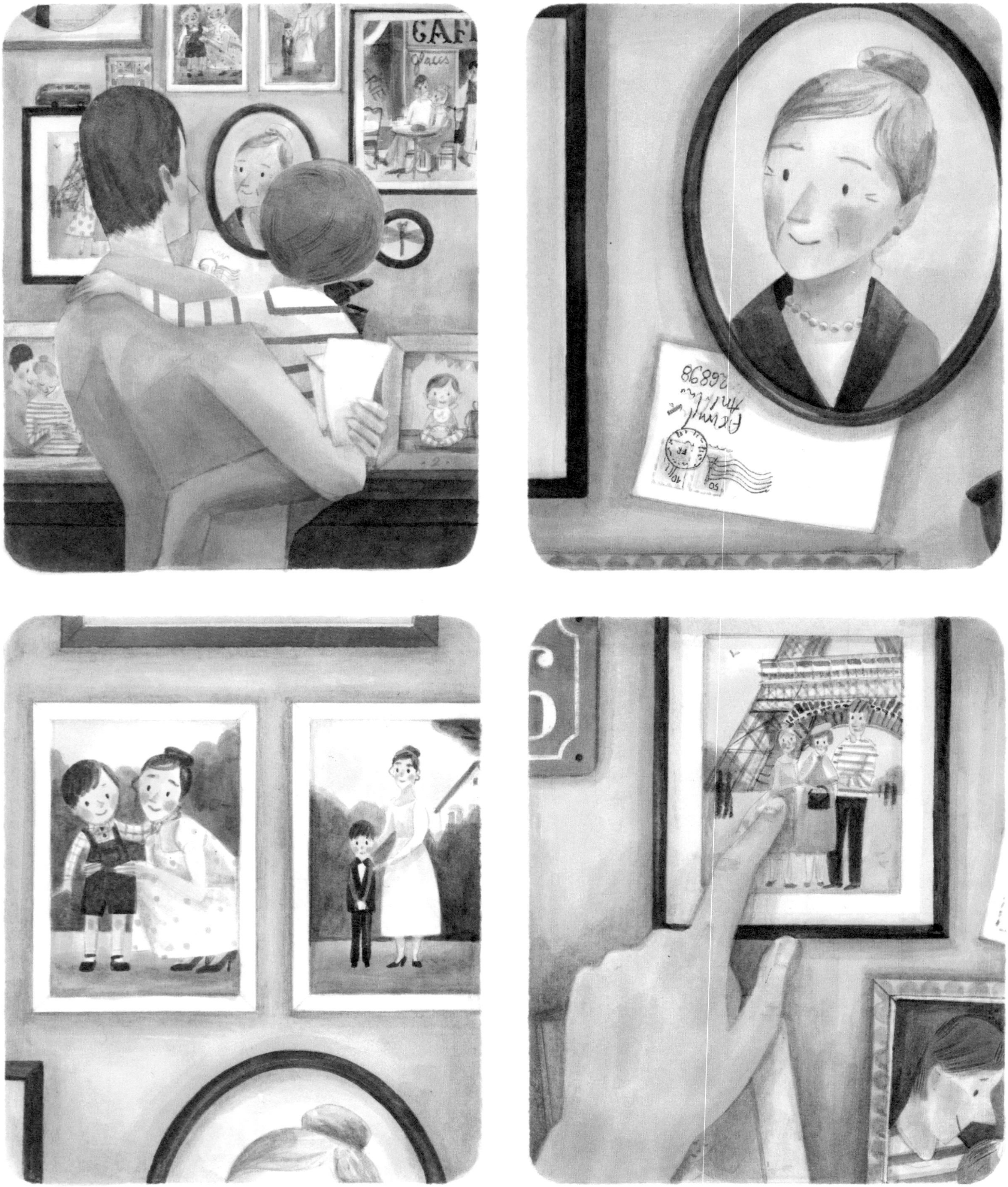

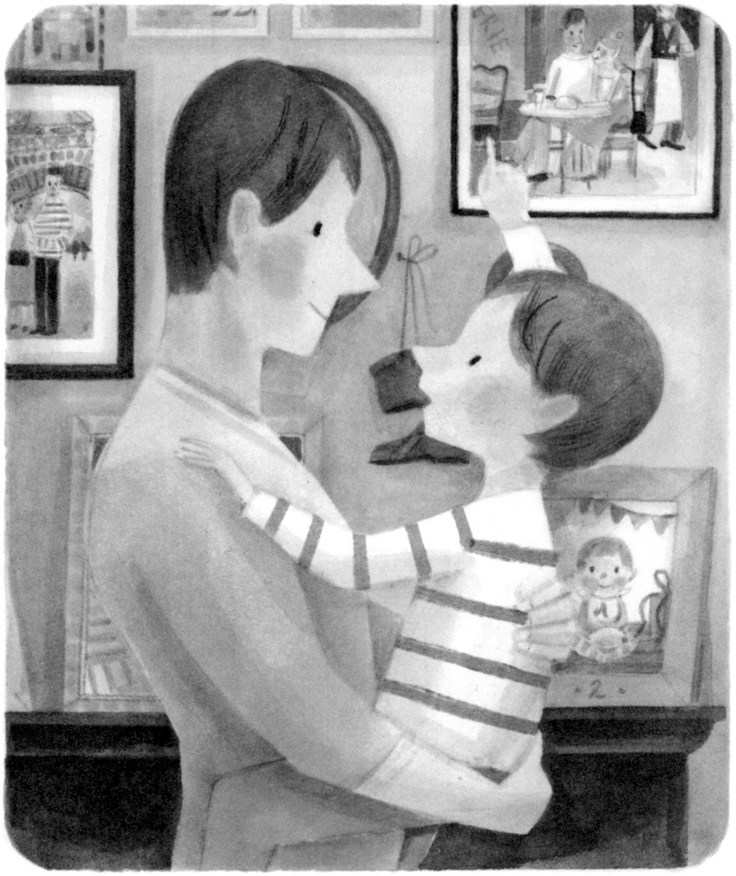

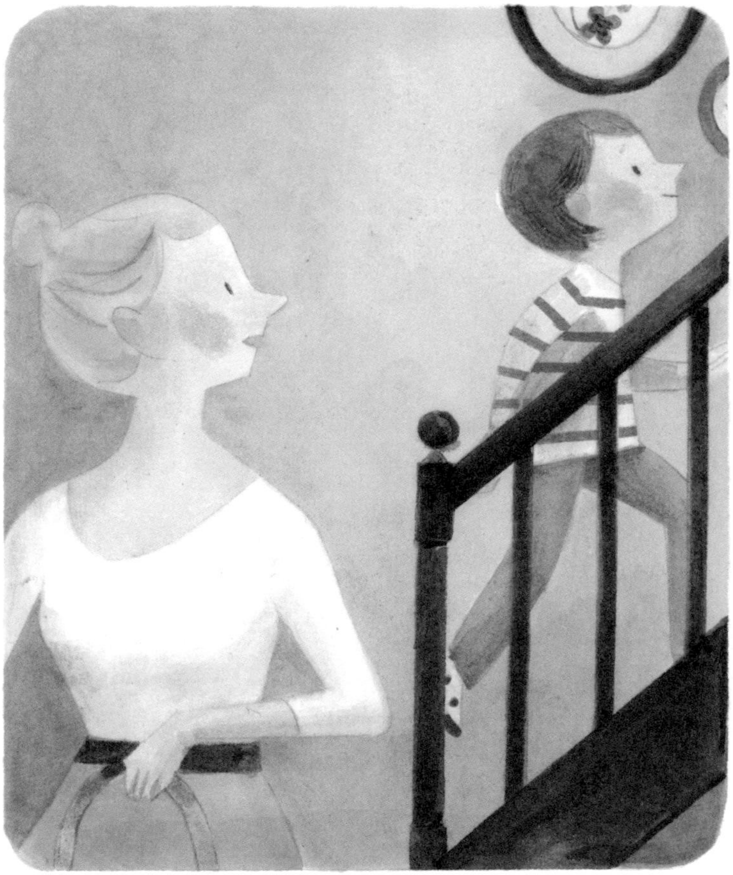

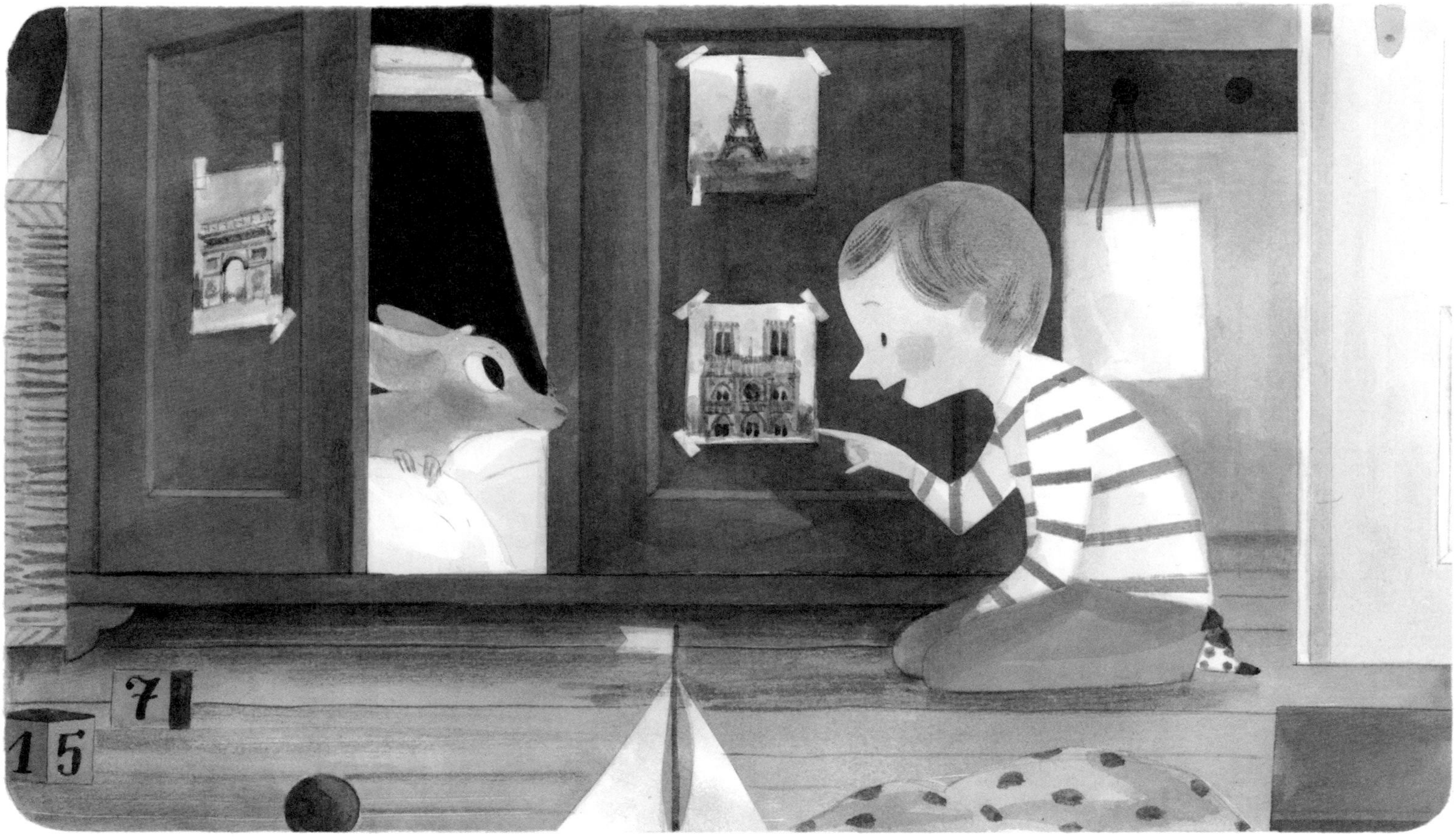
7
15

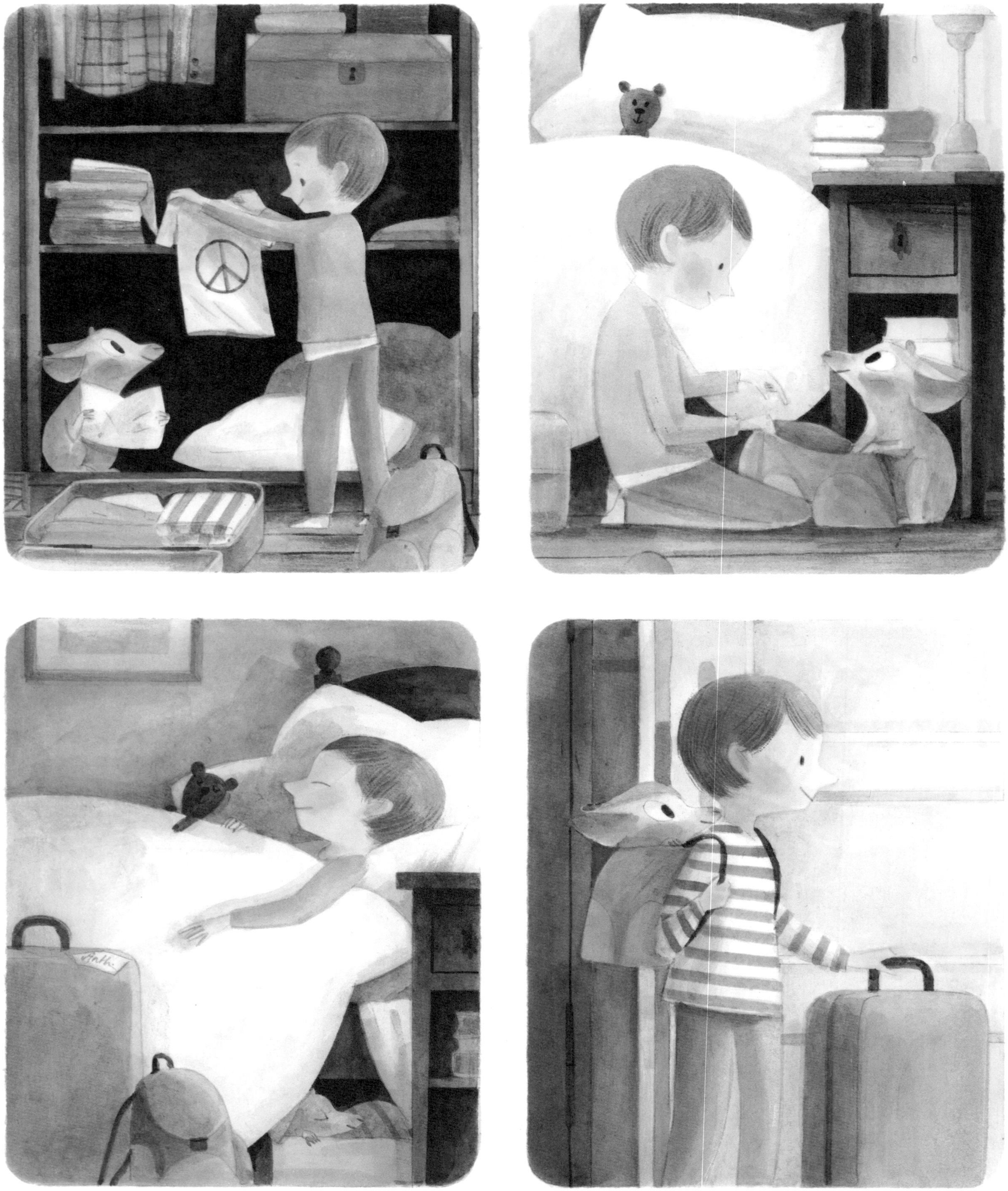

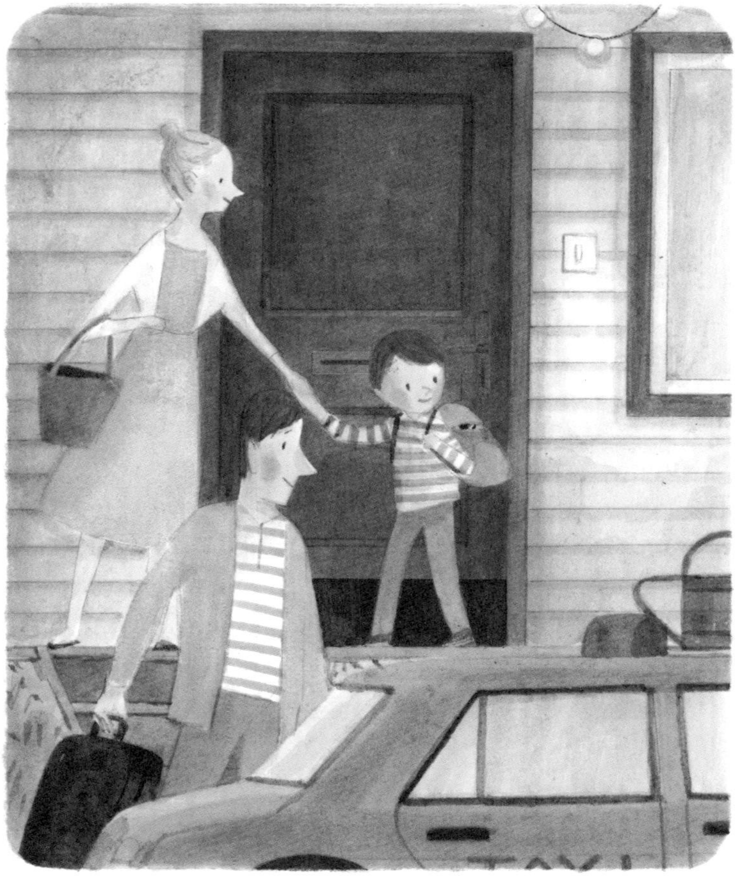
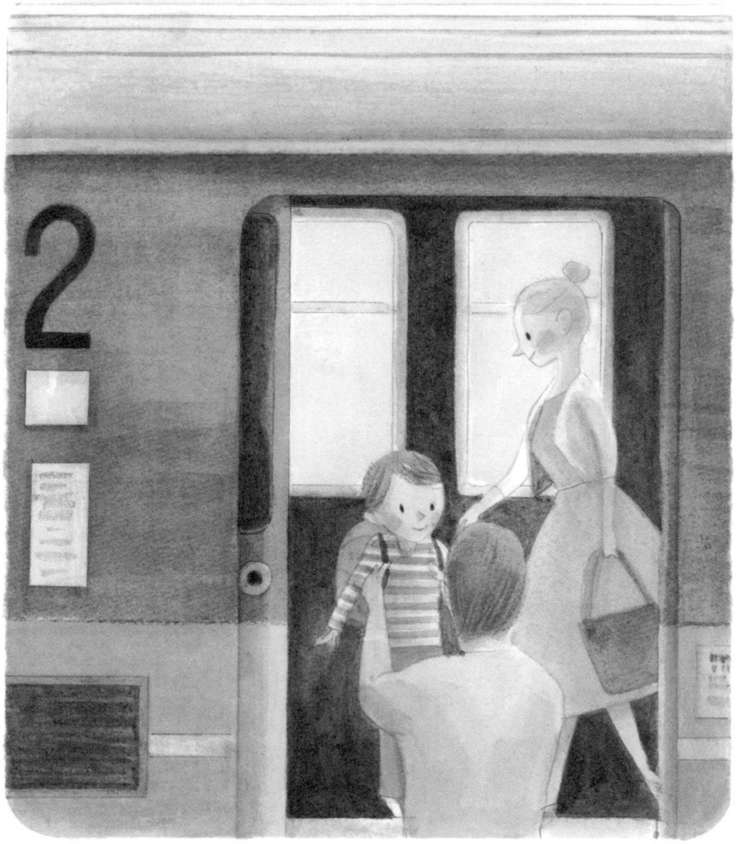
2
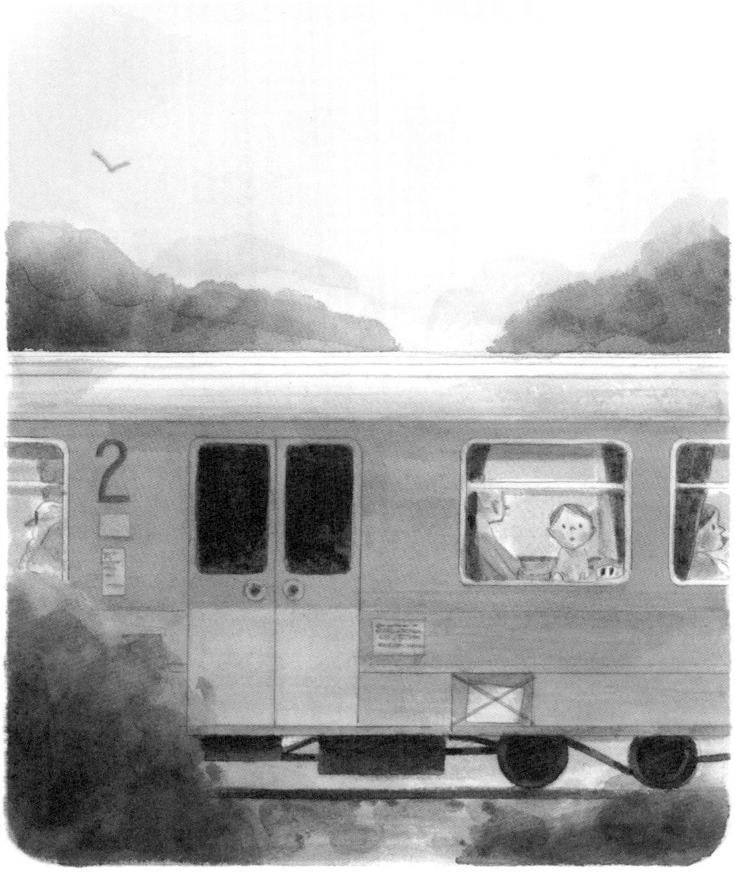
2
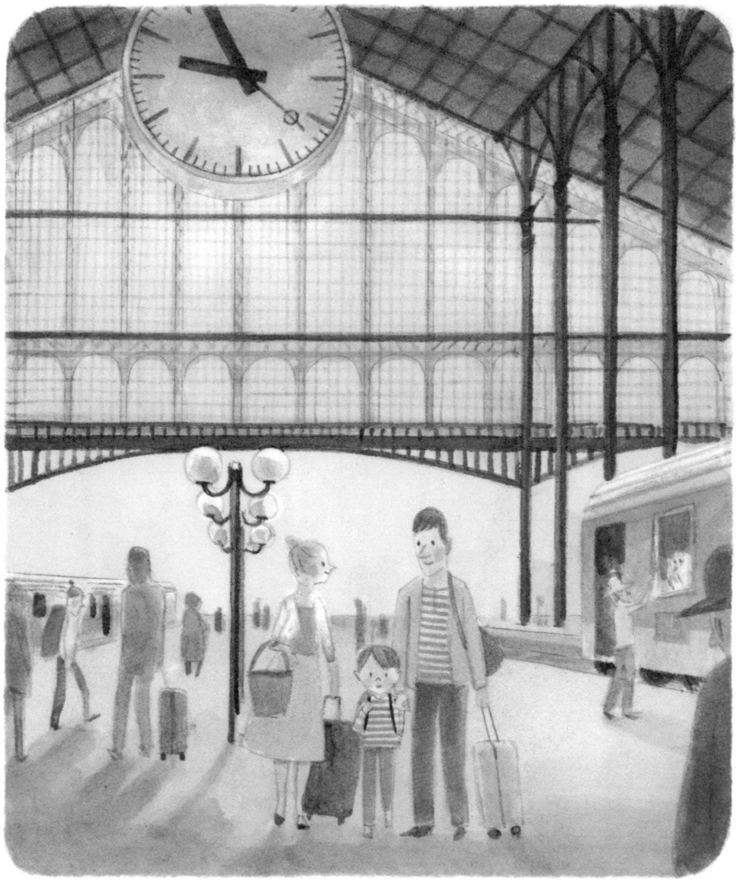

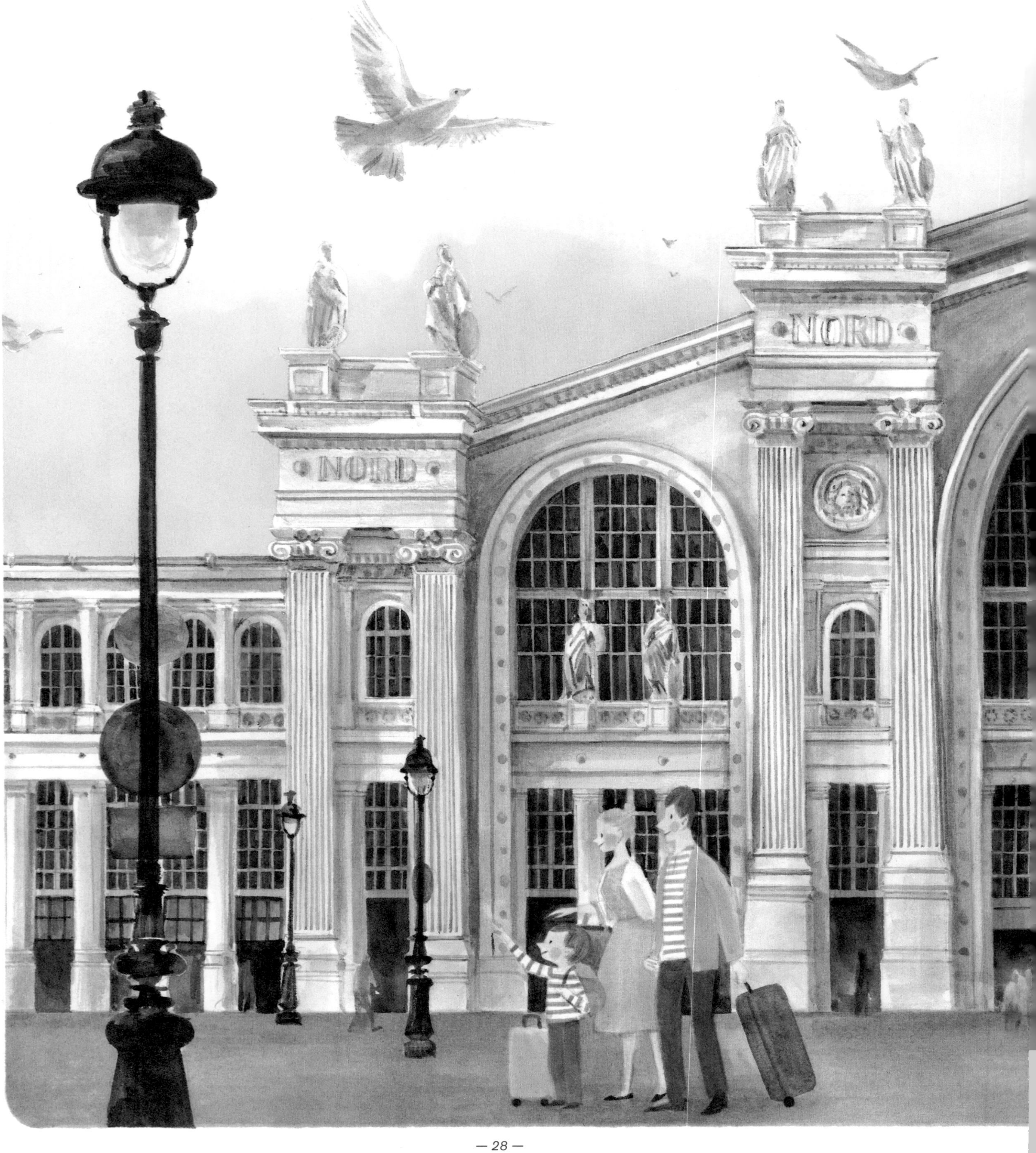
NORD
NORD

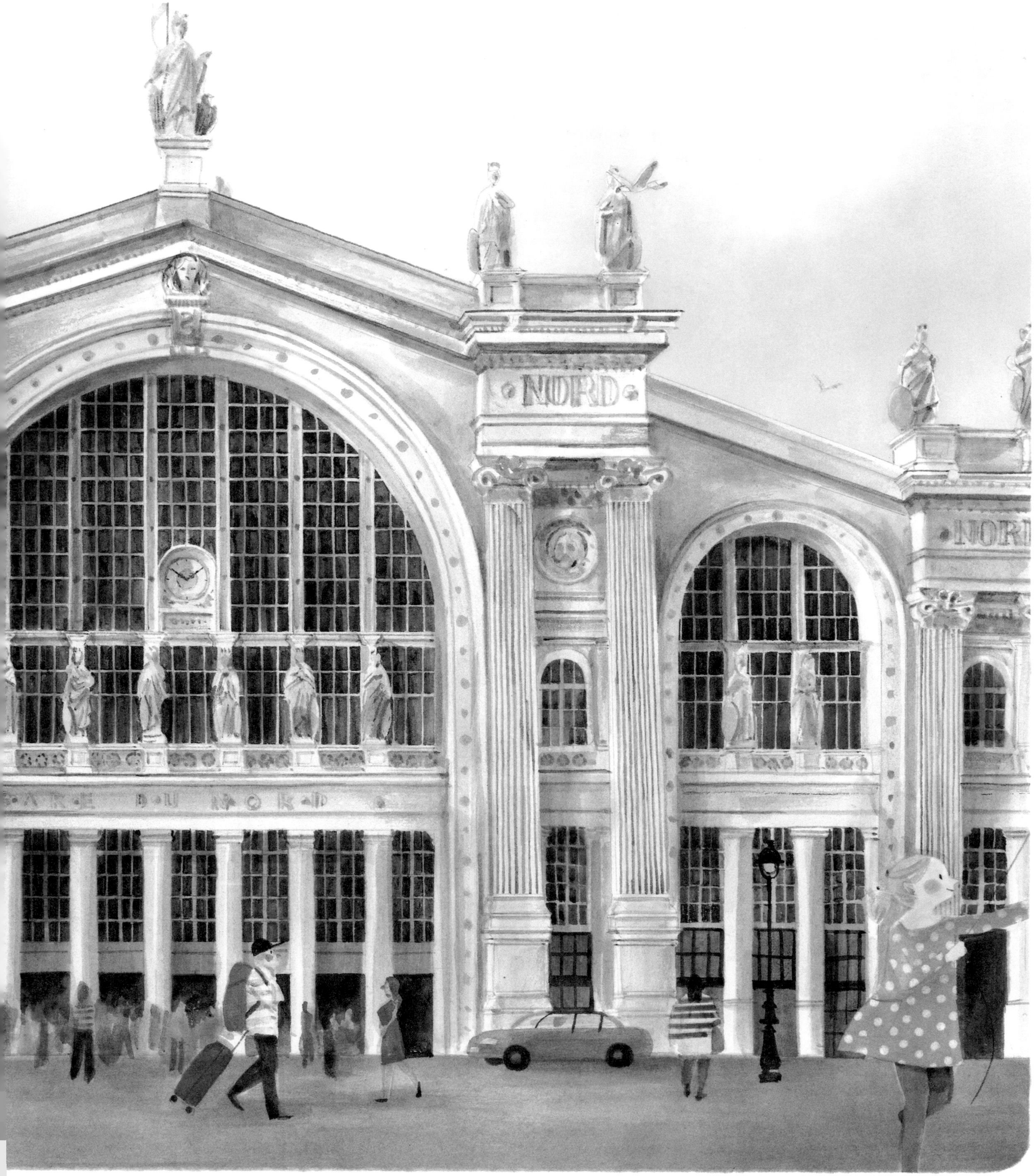
NORD

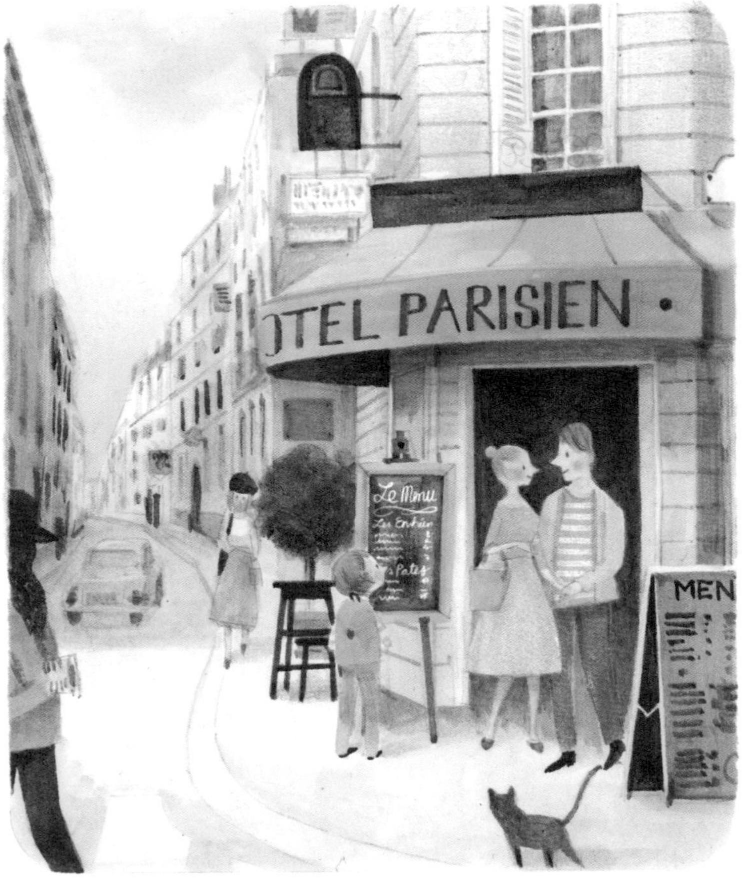
OTEL PARISIEN
Le Menu
MEN

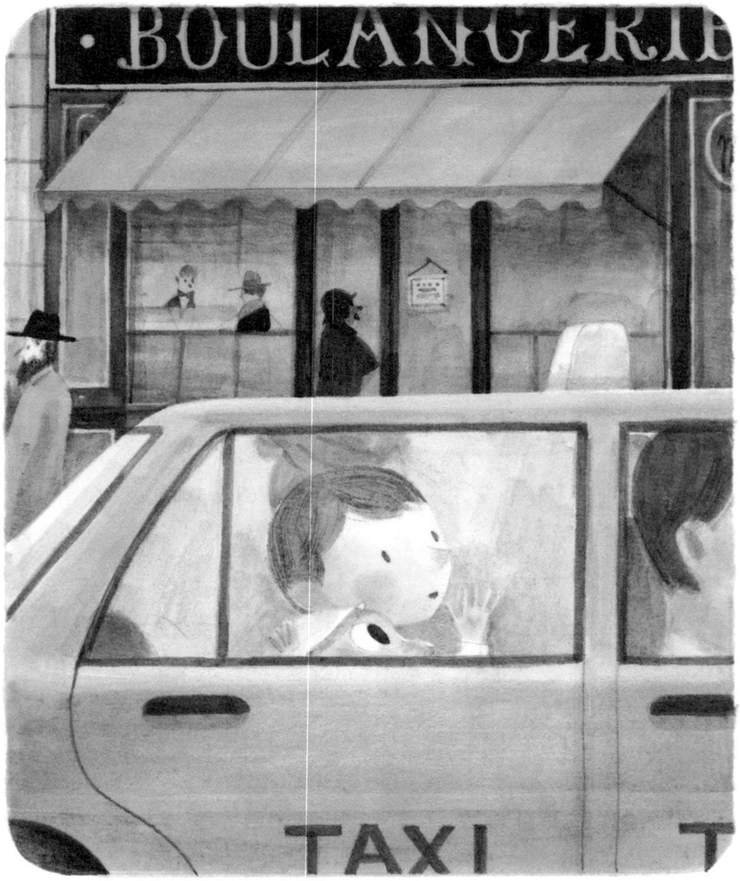
BOULANGERI
TAXI

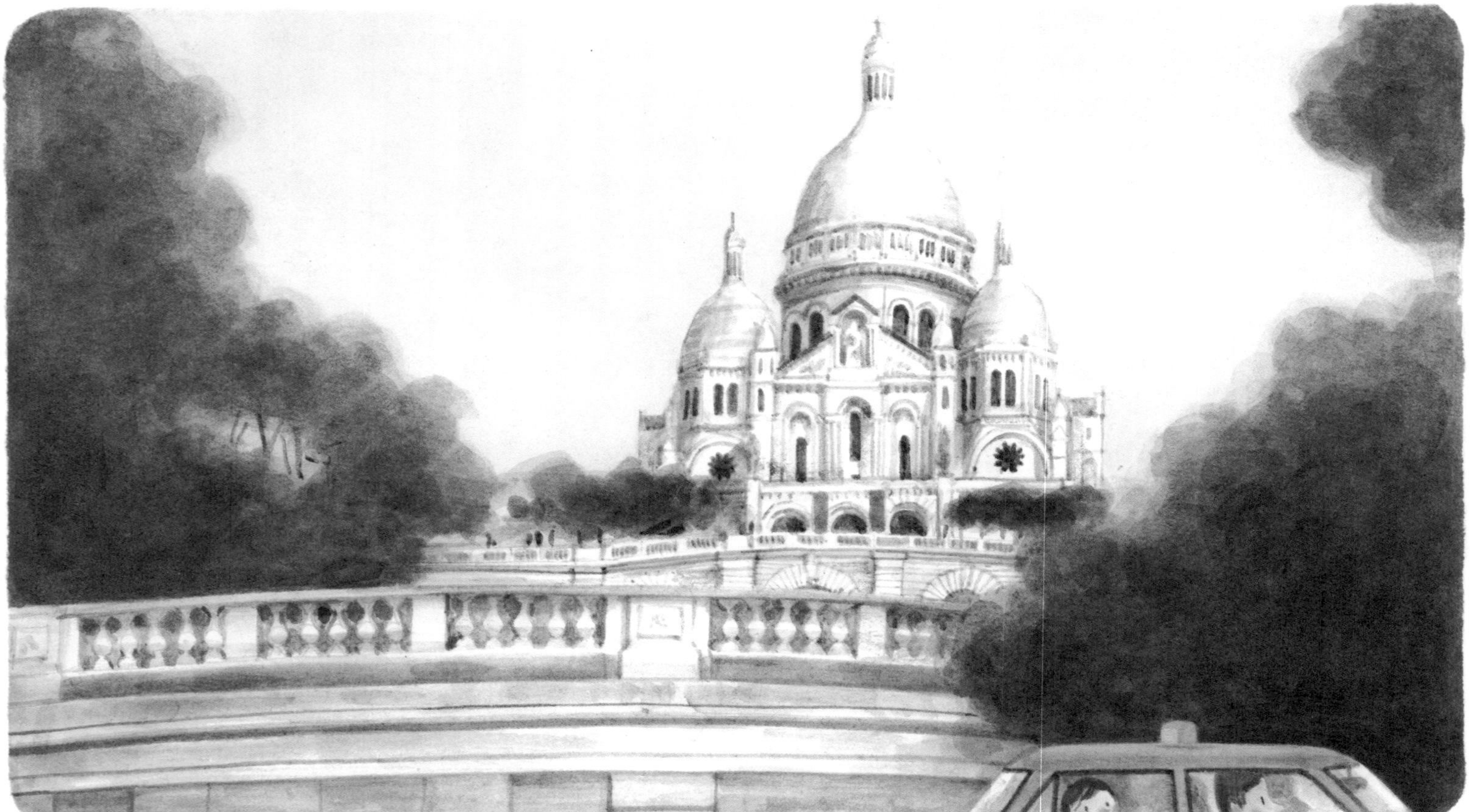

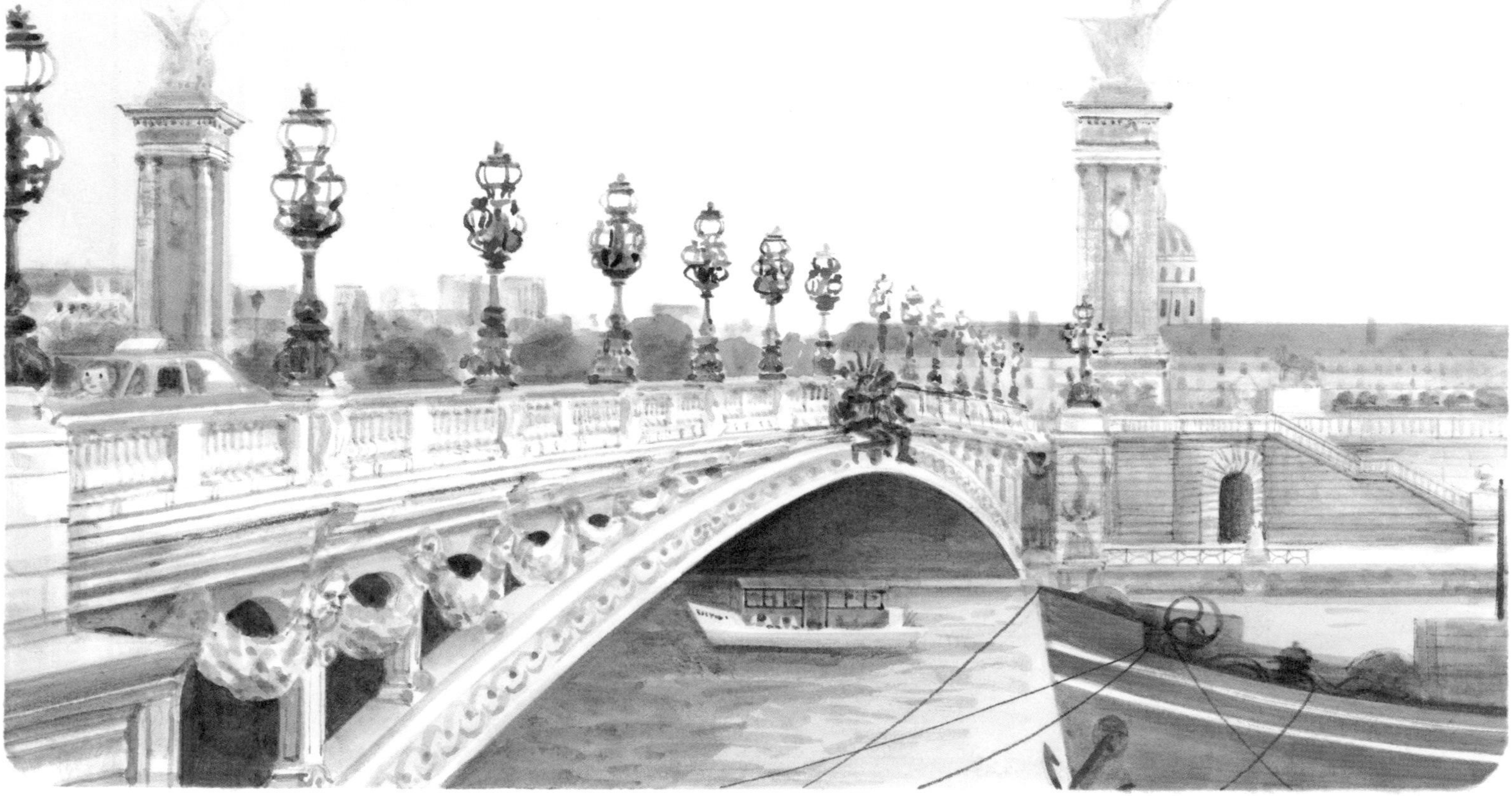

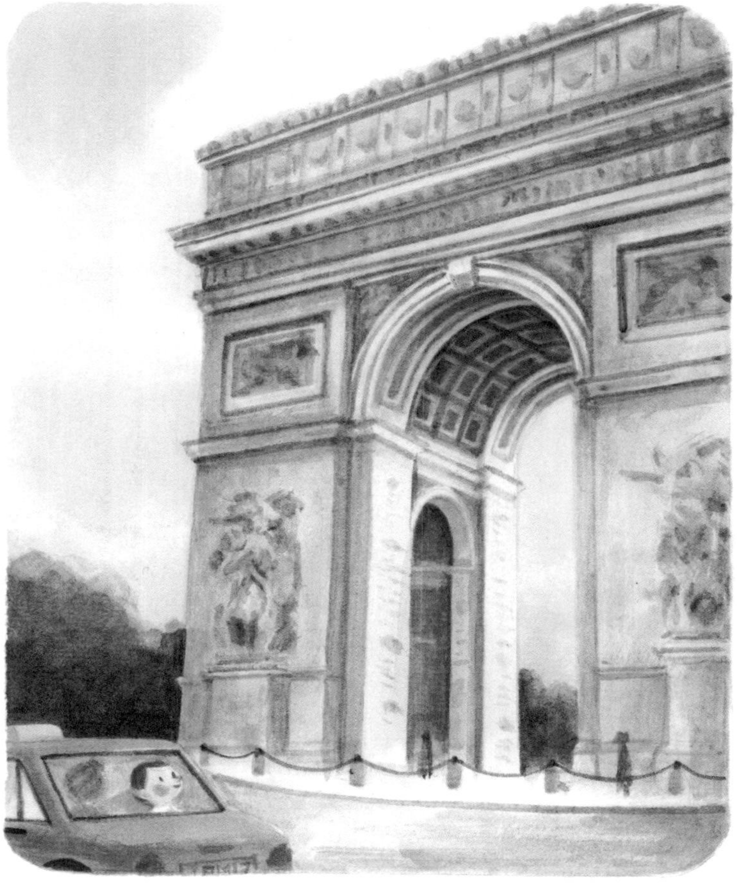

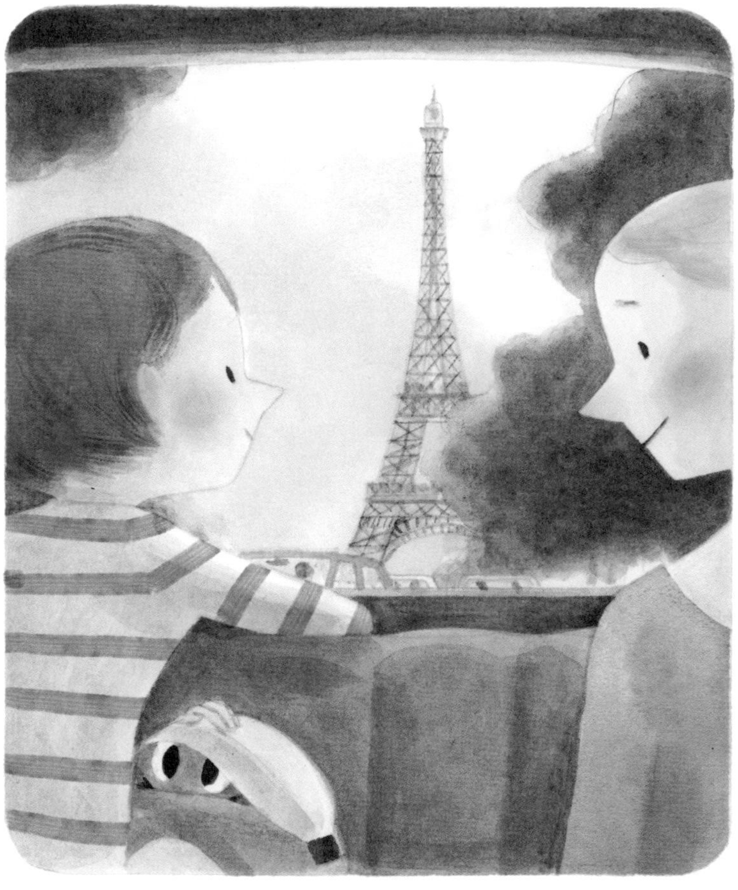

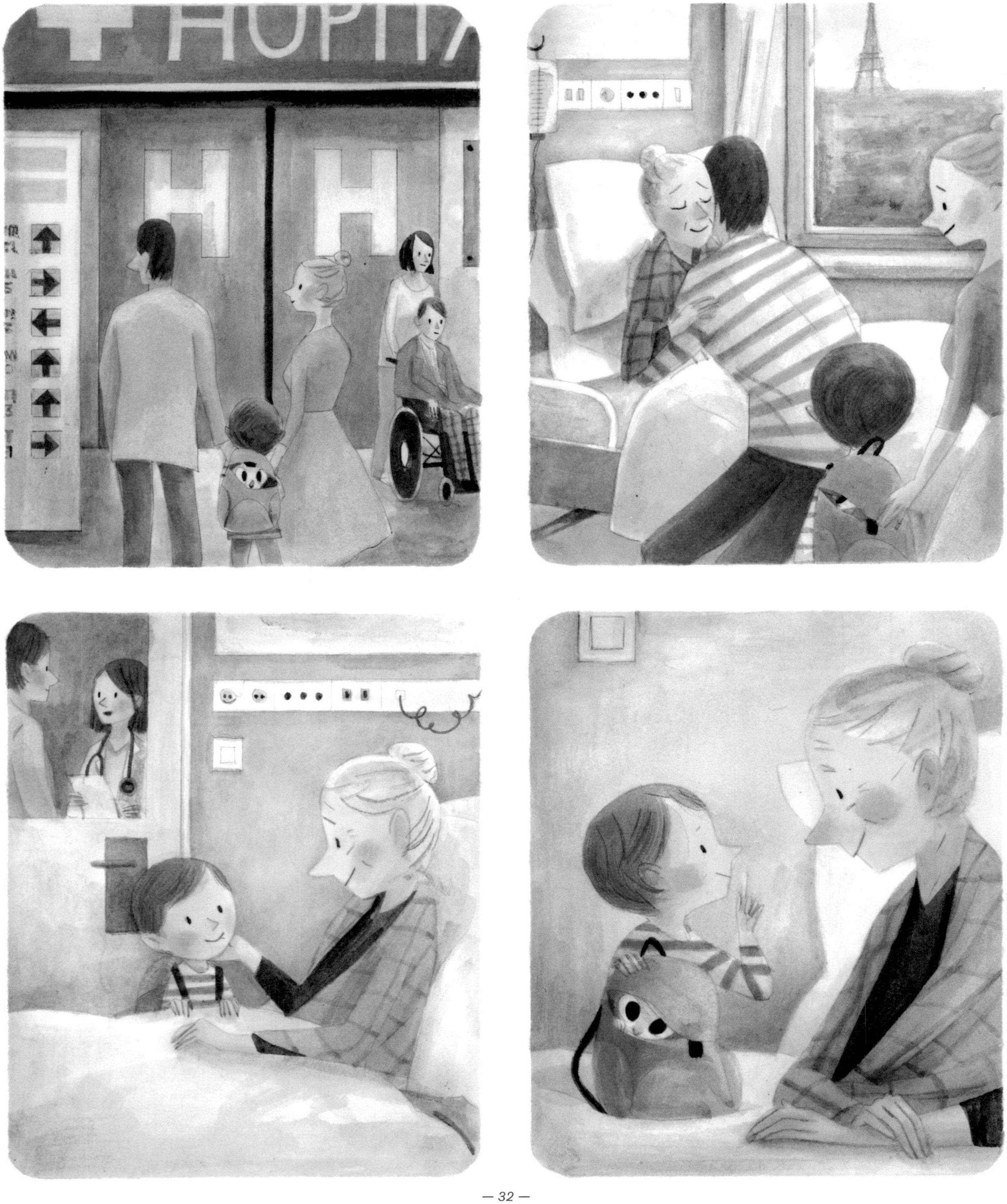
HOPIT

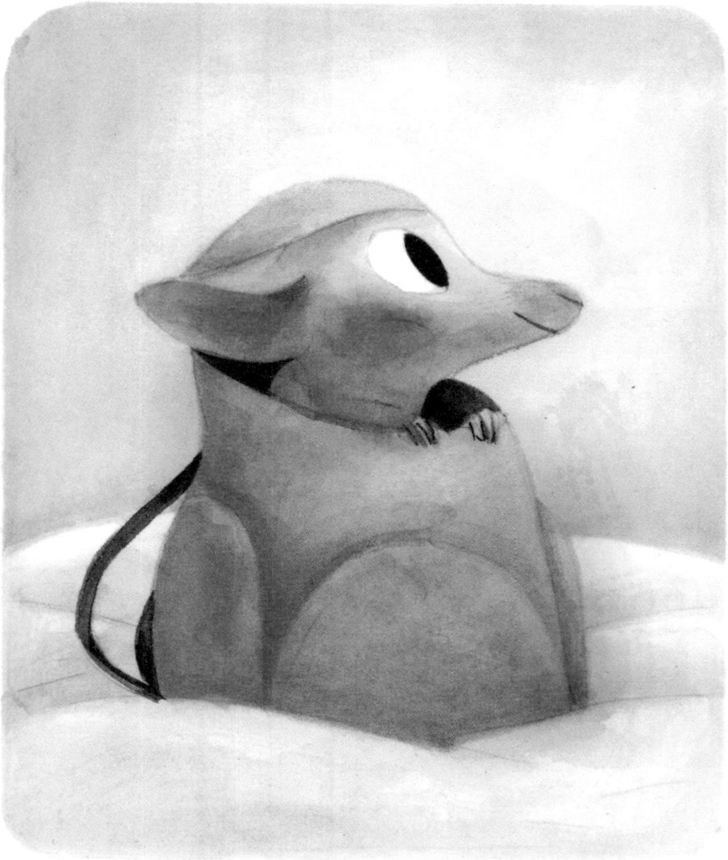
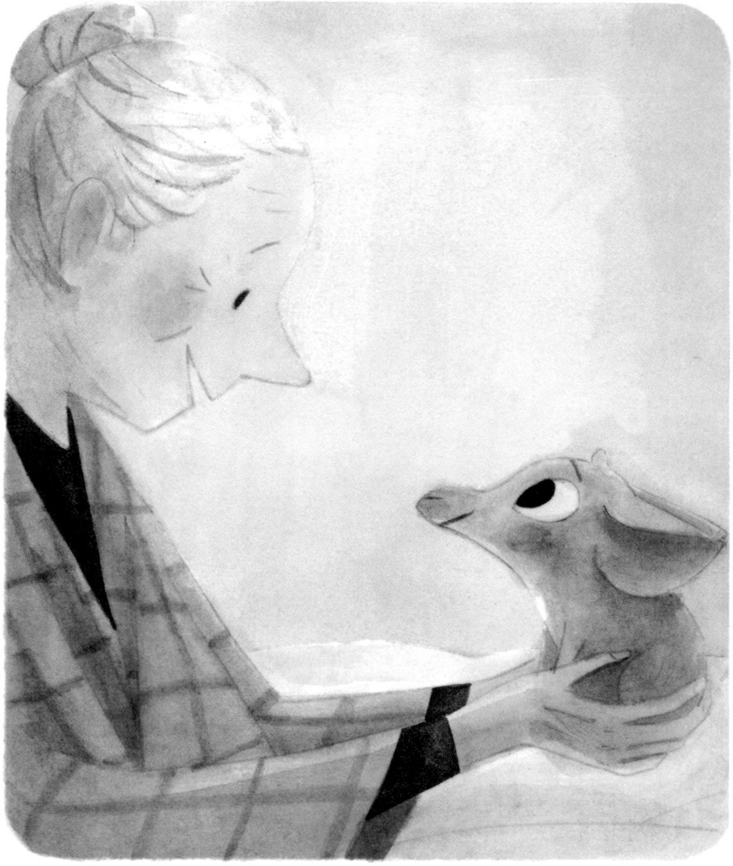
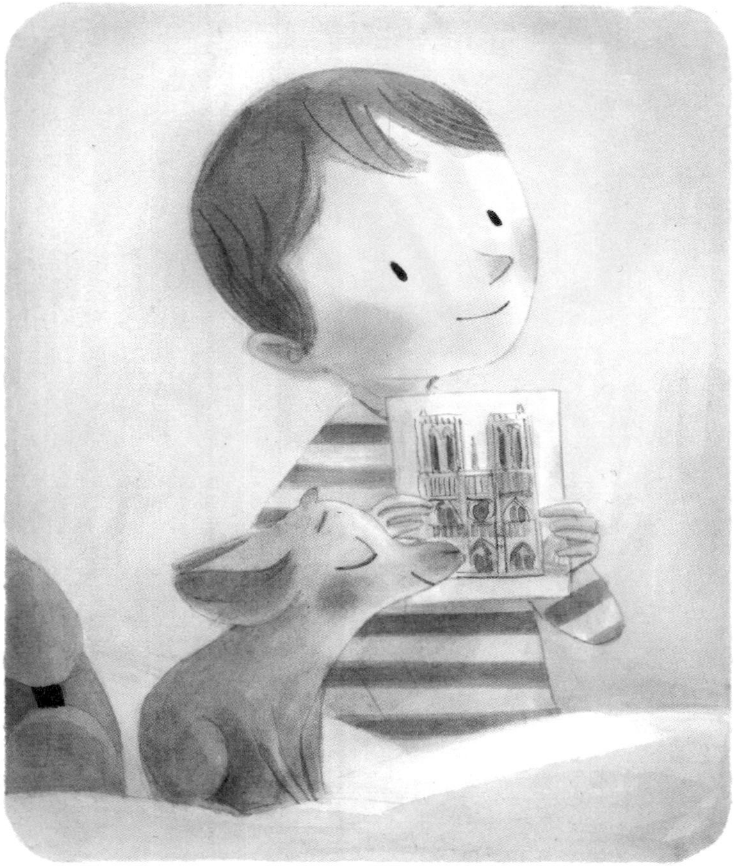
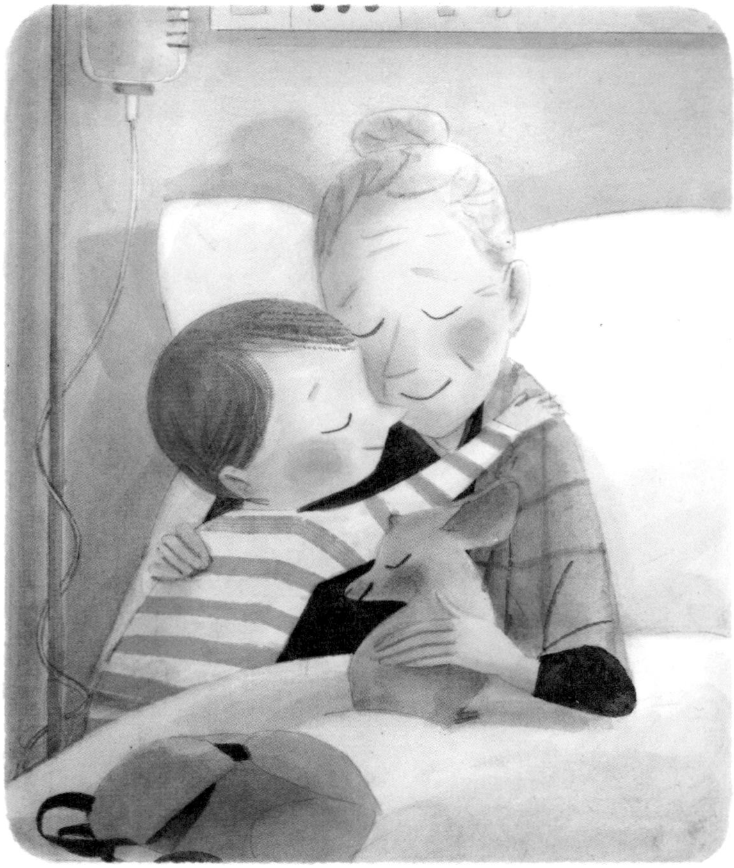

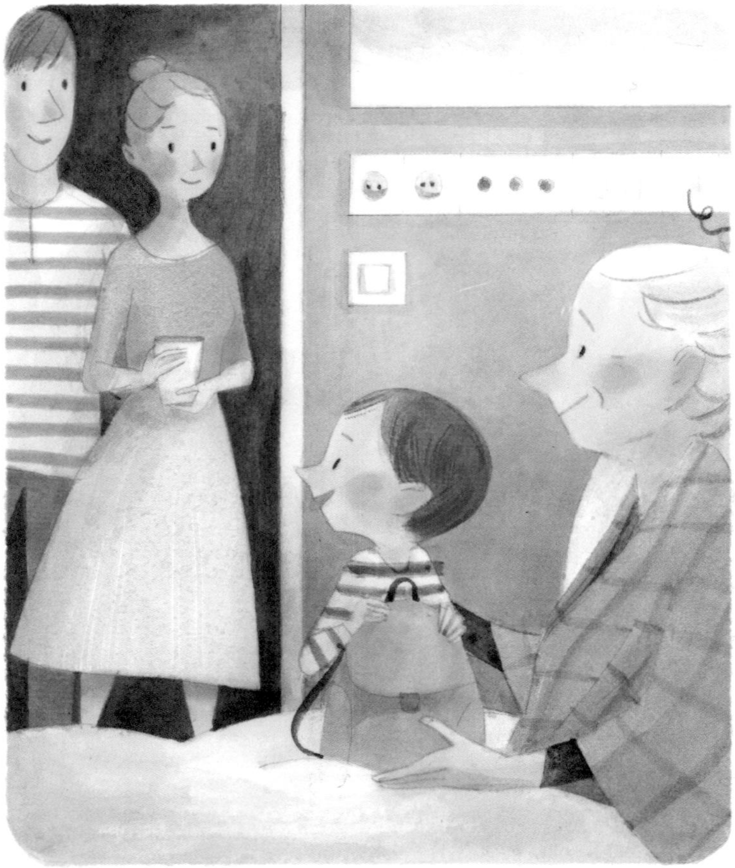

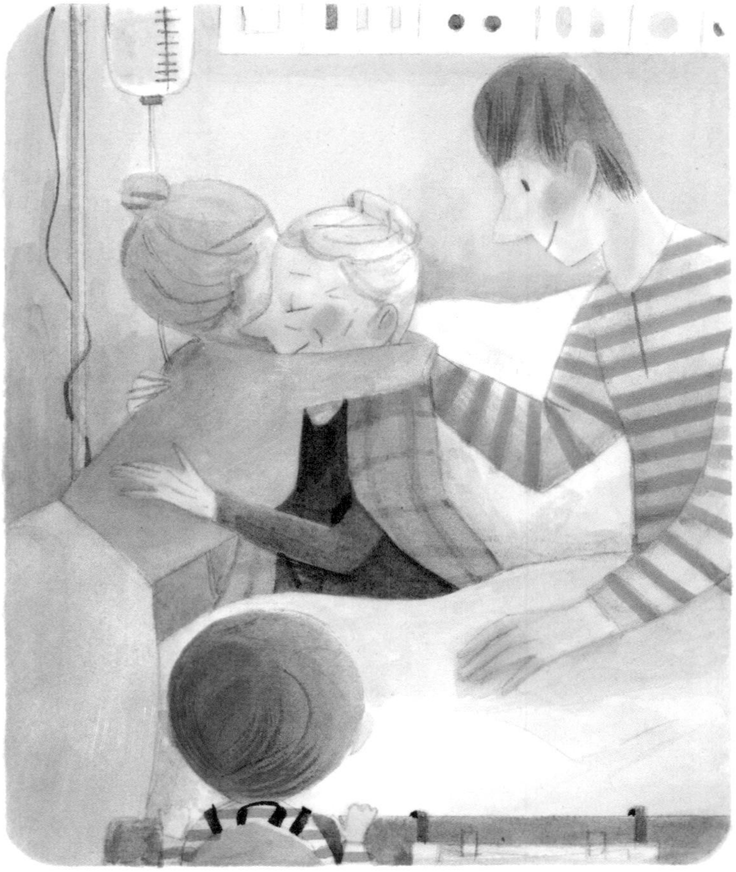

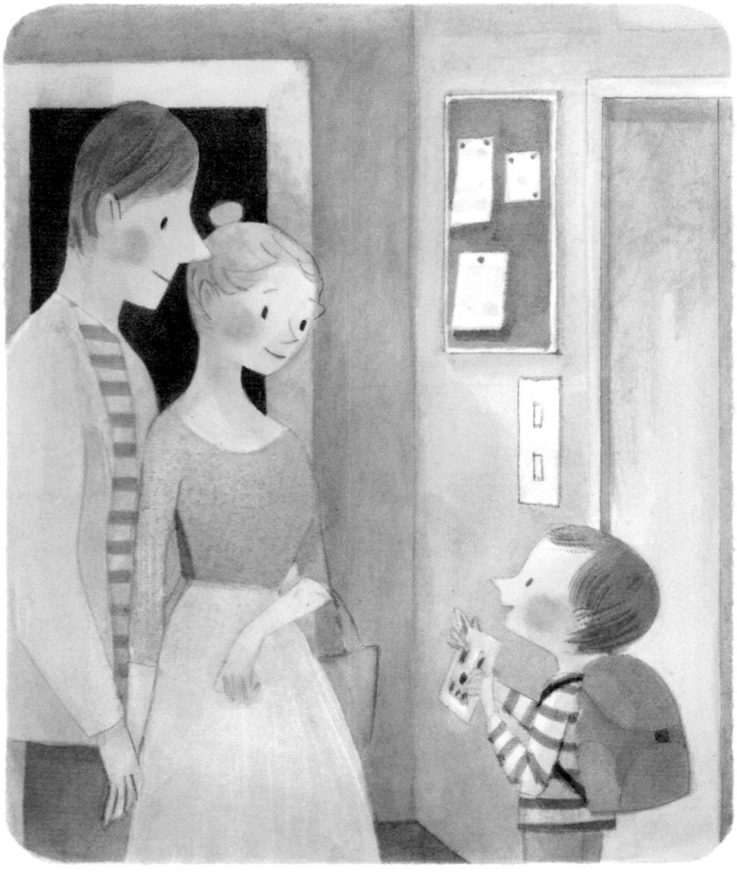

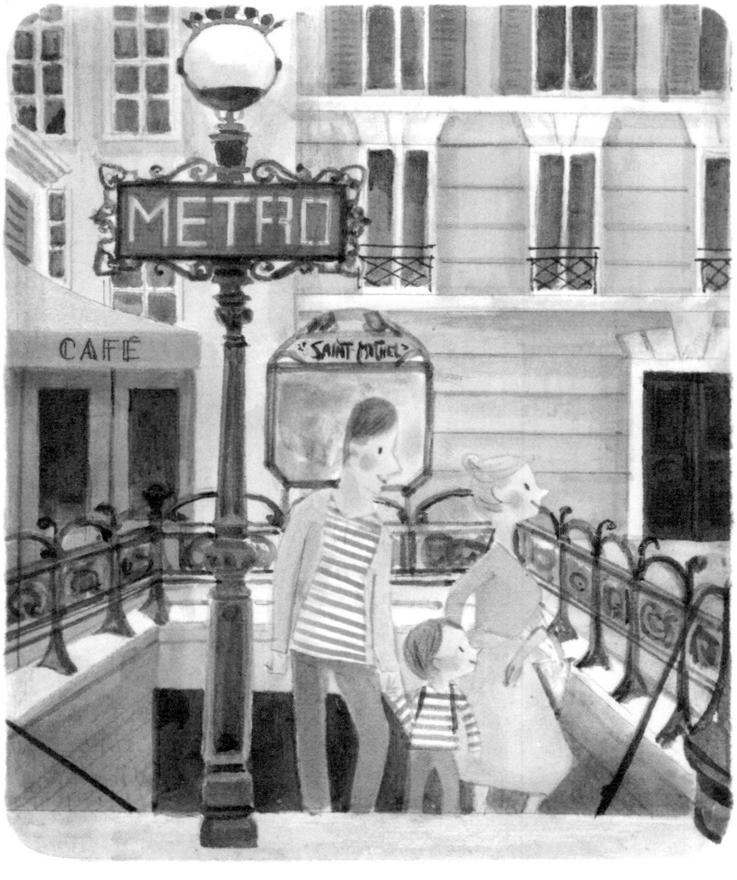
METRO
CAFÉ
SAINT-MICHEL

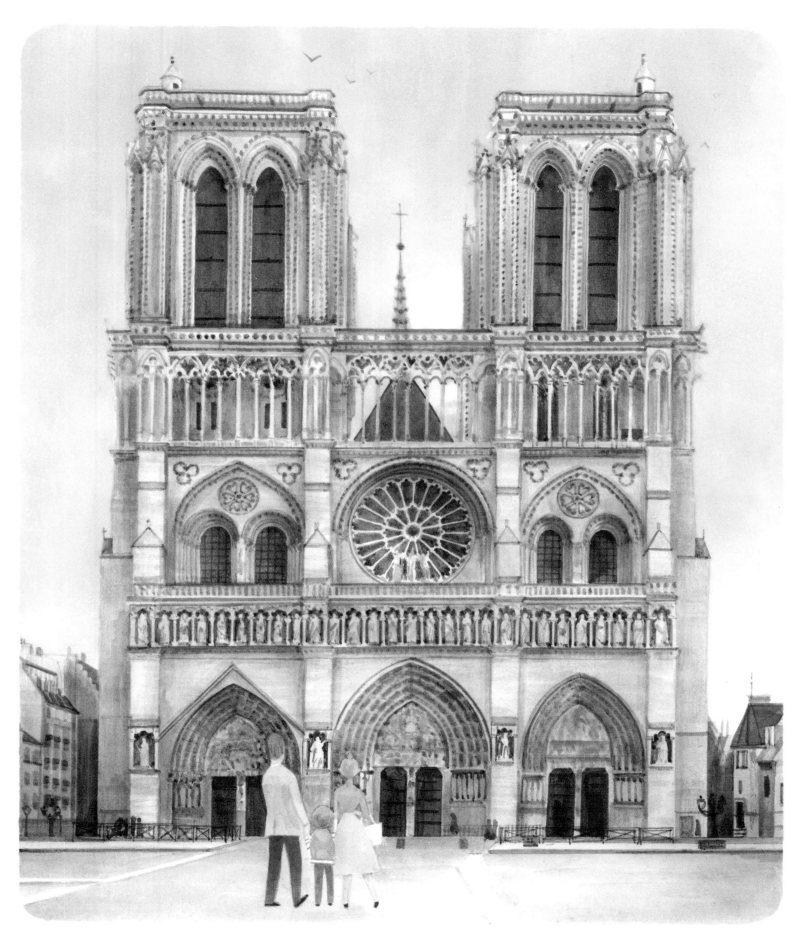

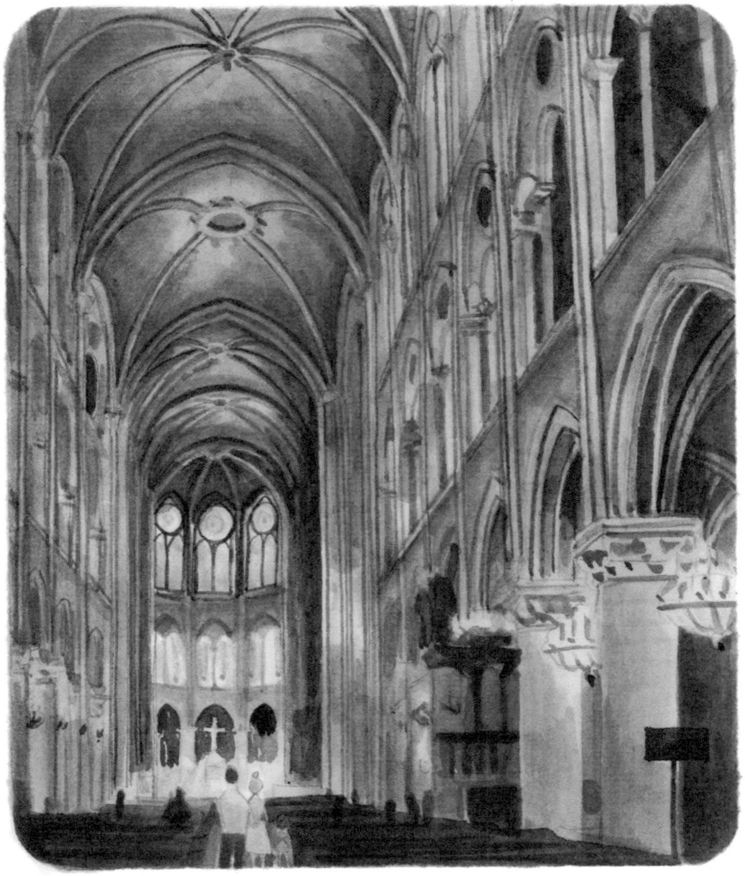
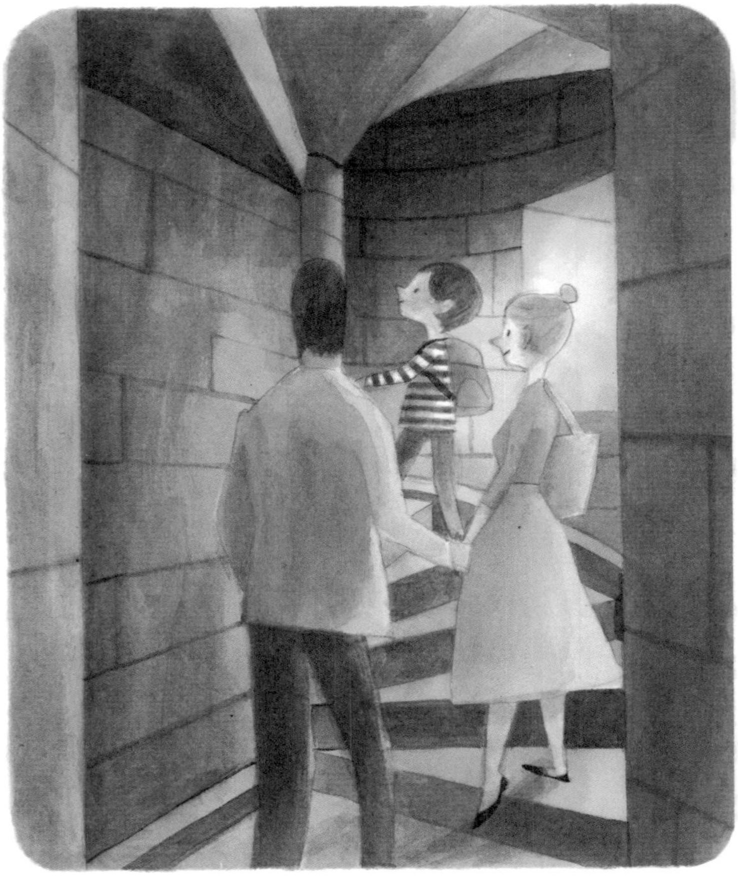
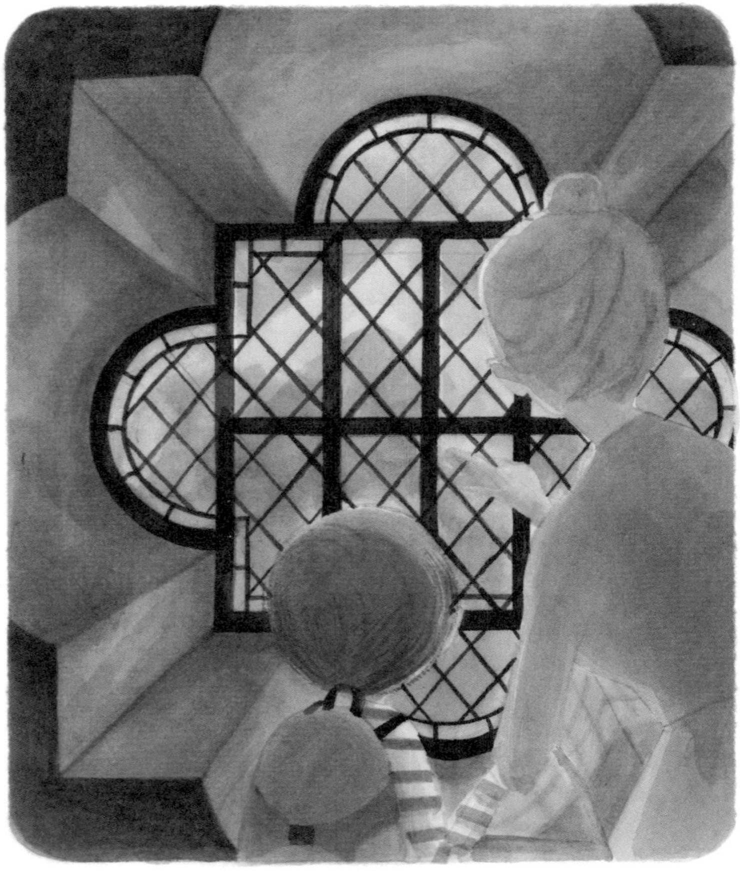
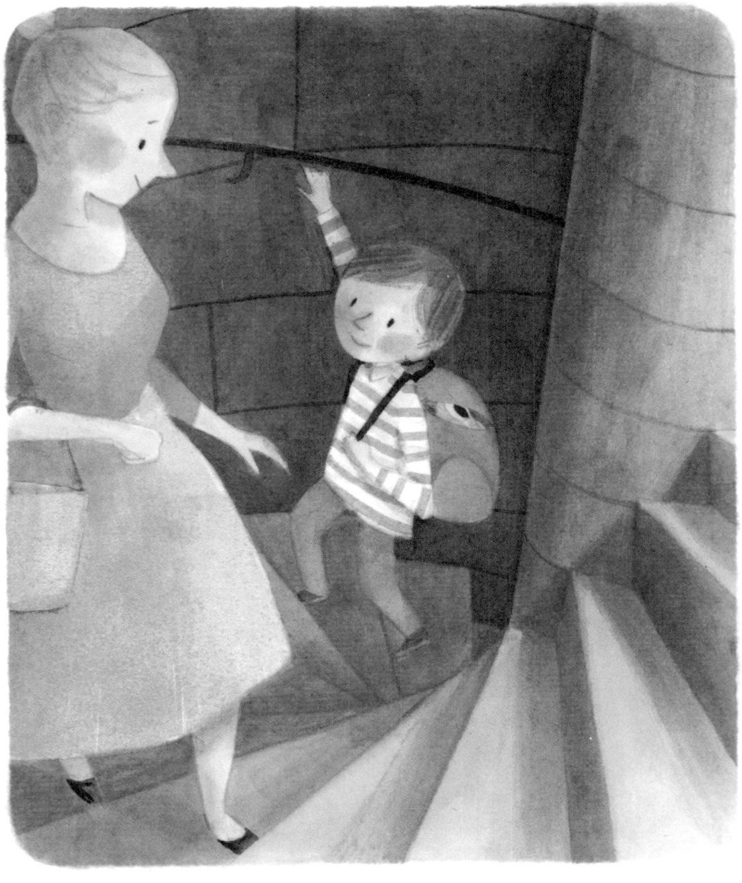

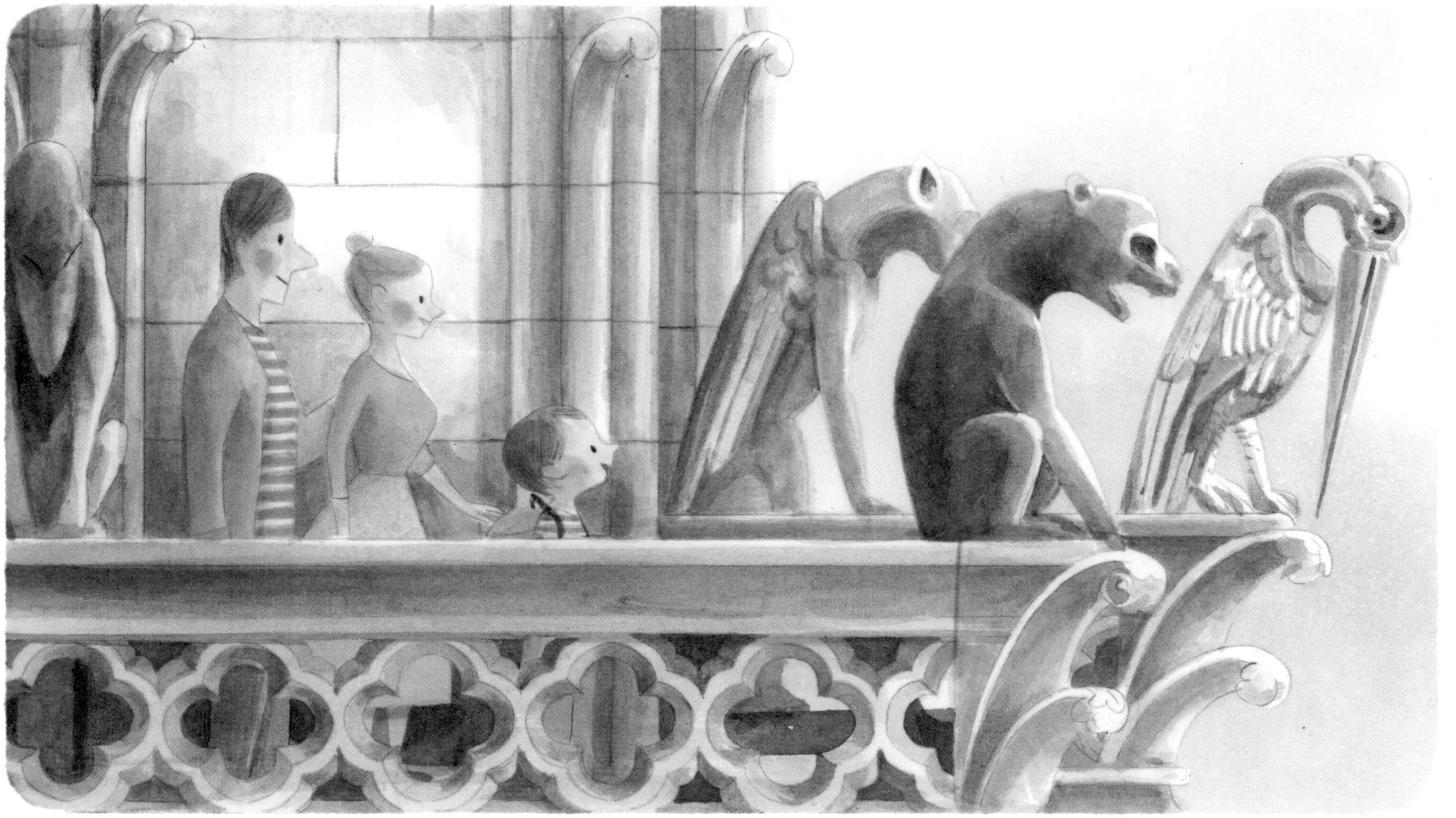

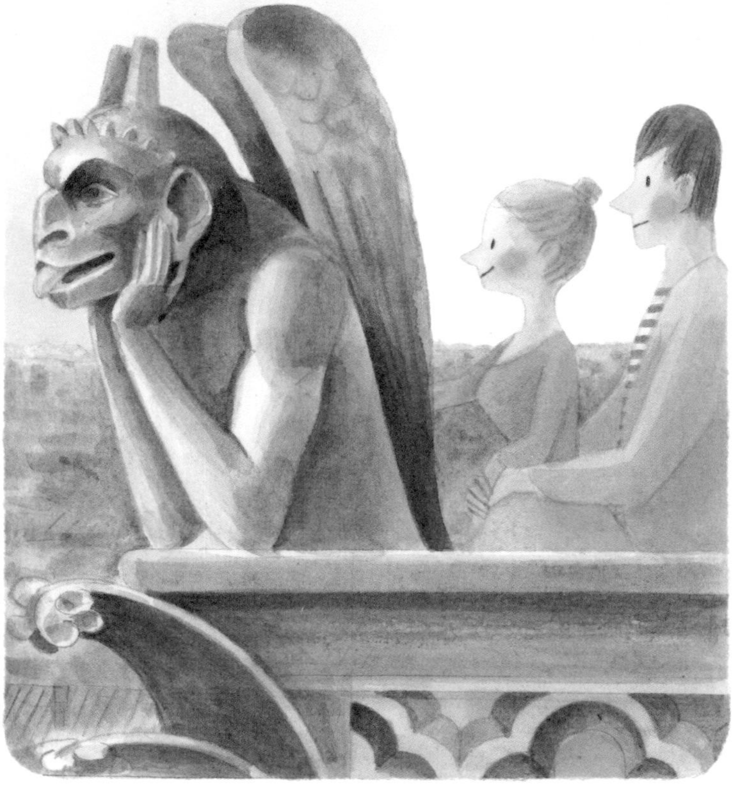

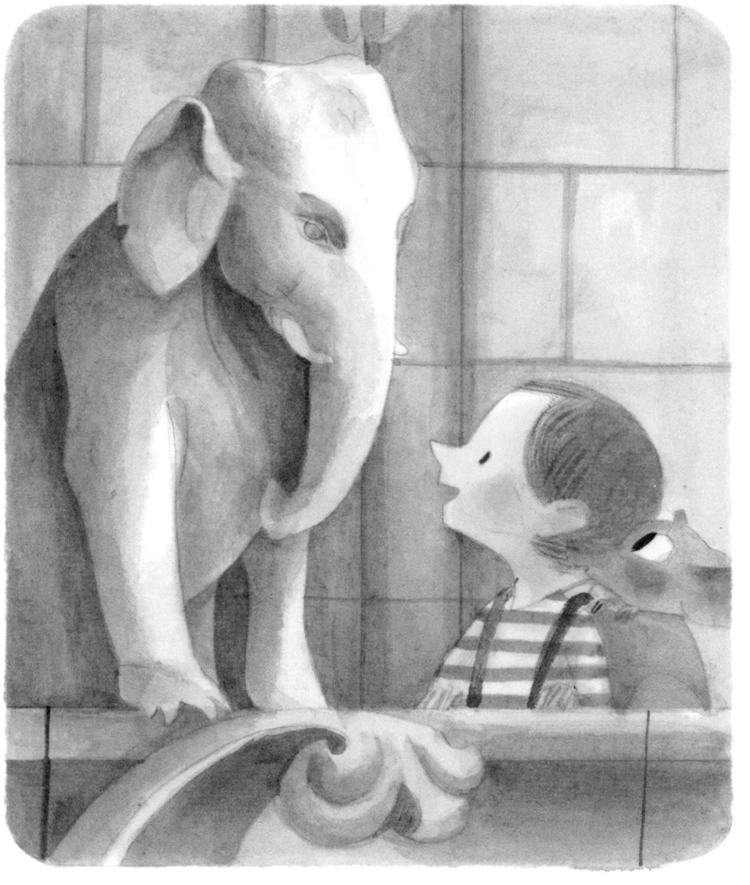

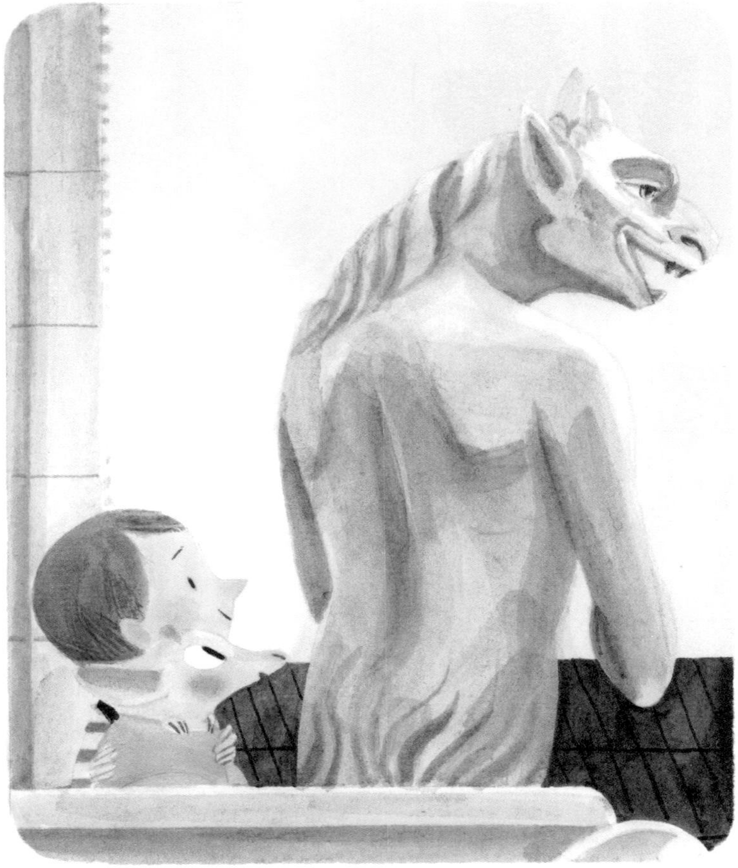

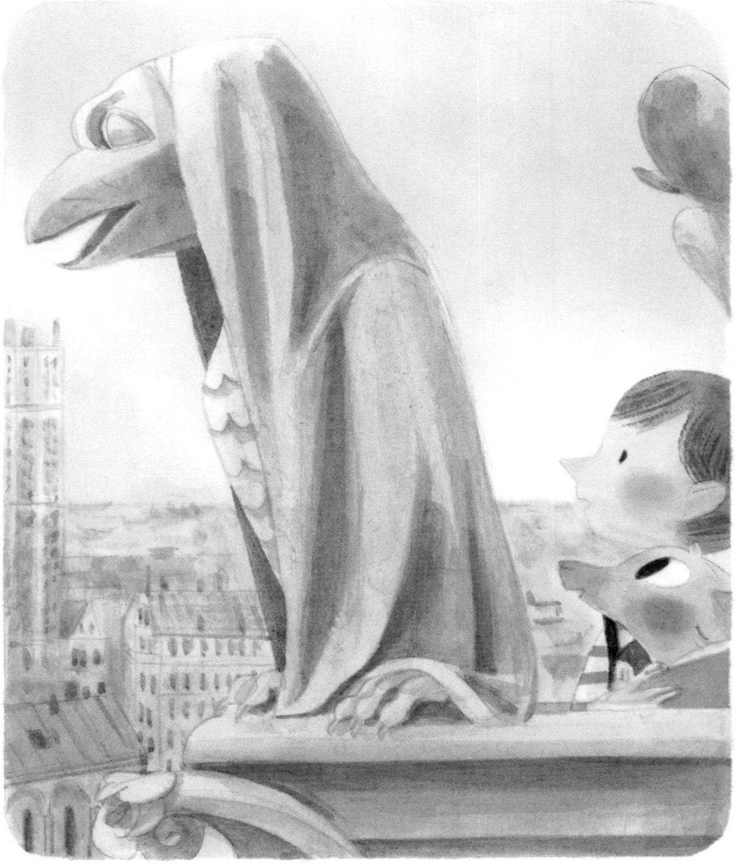

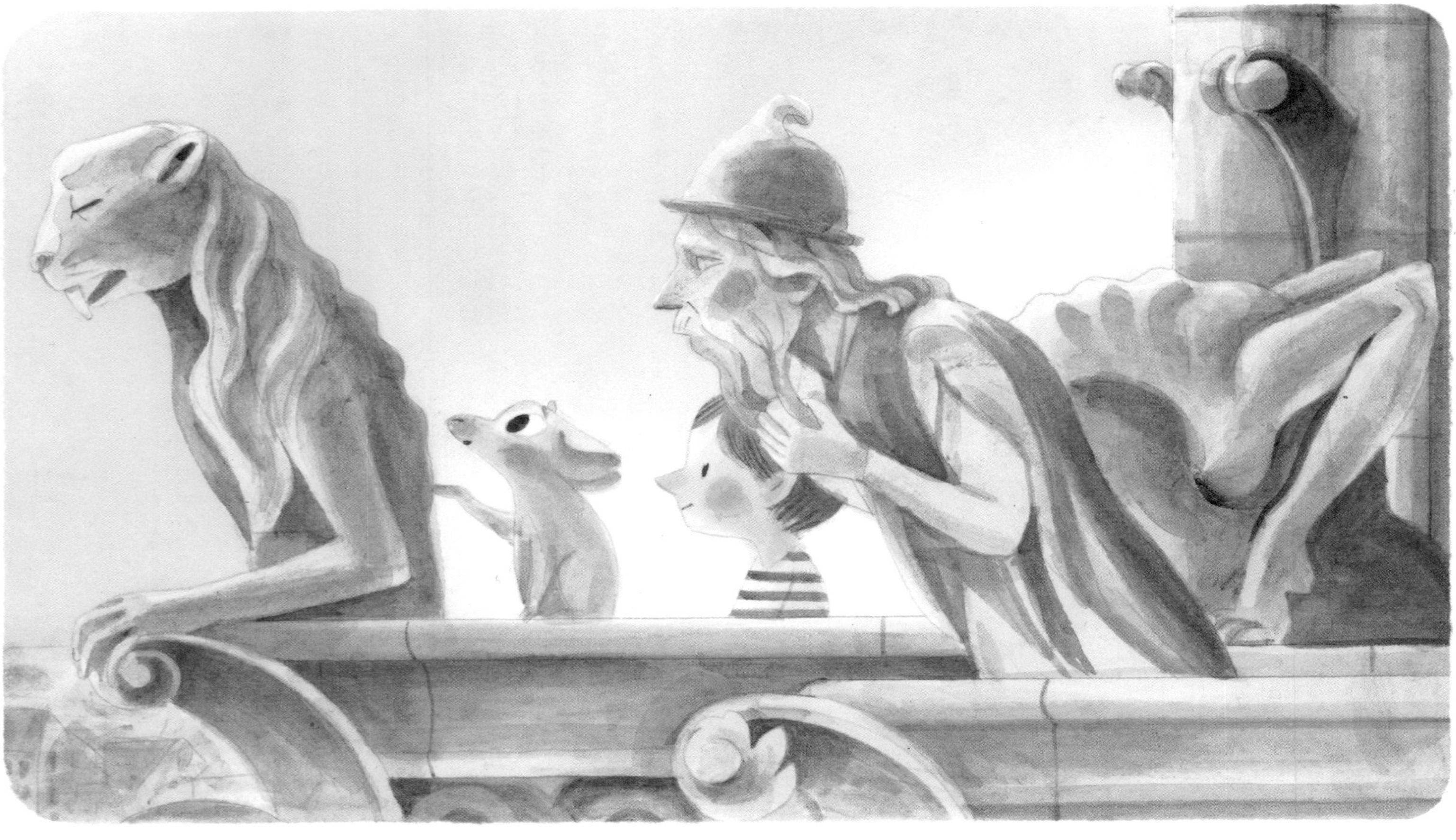

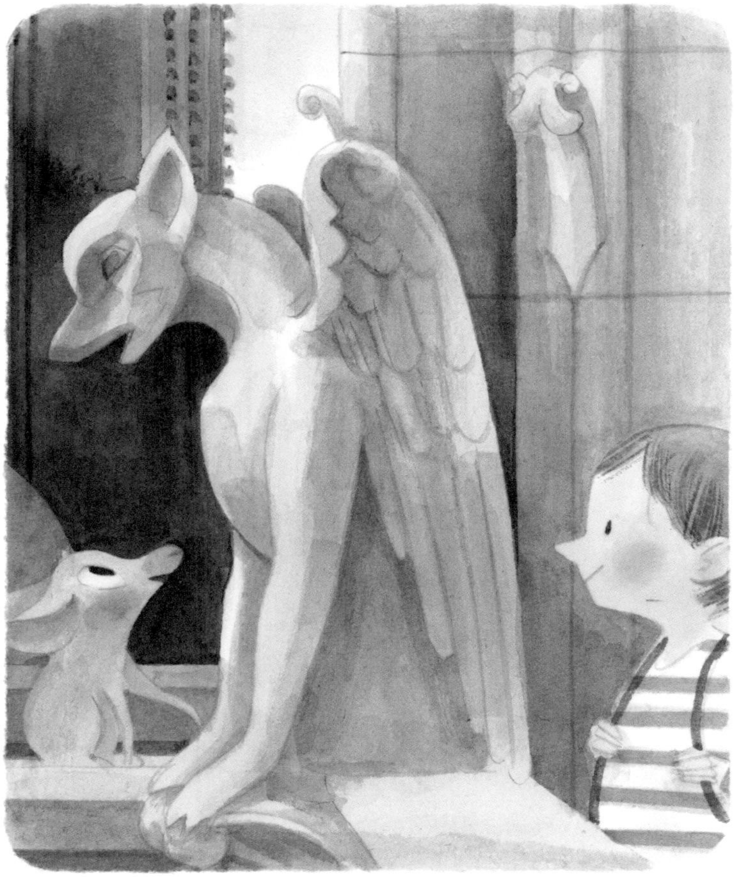

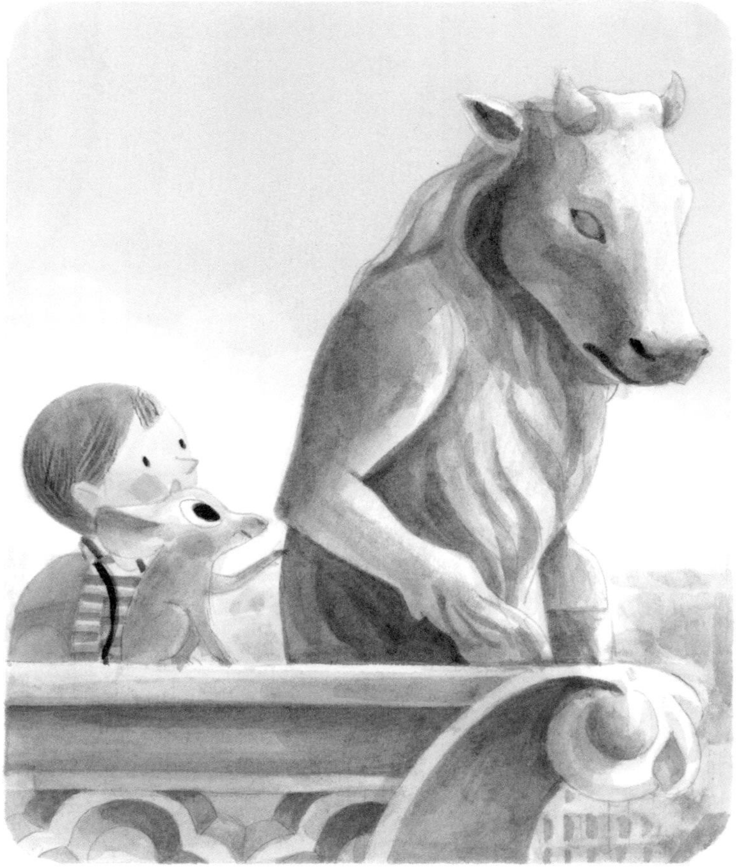

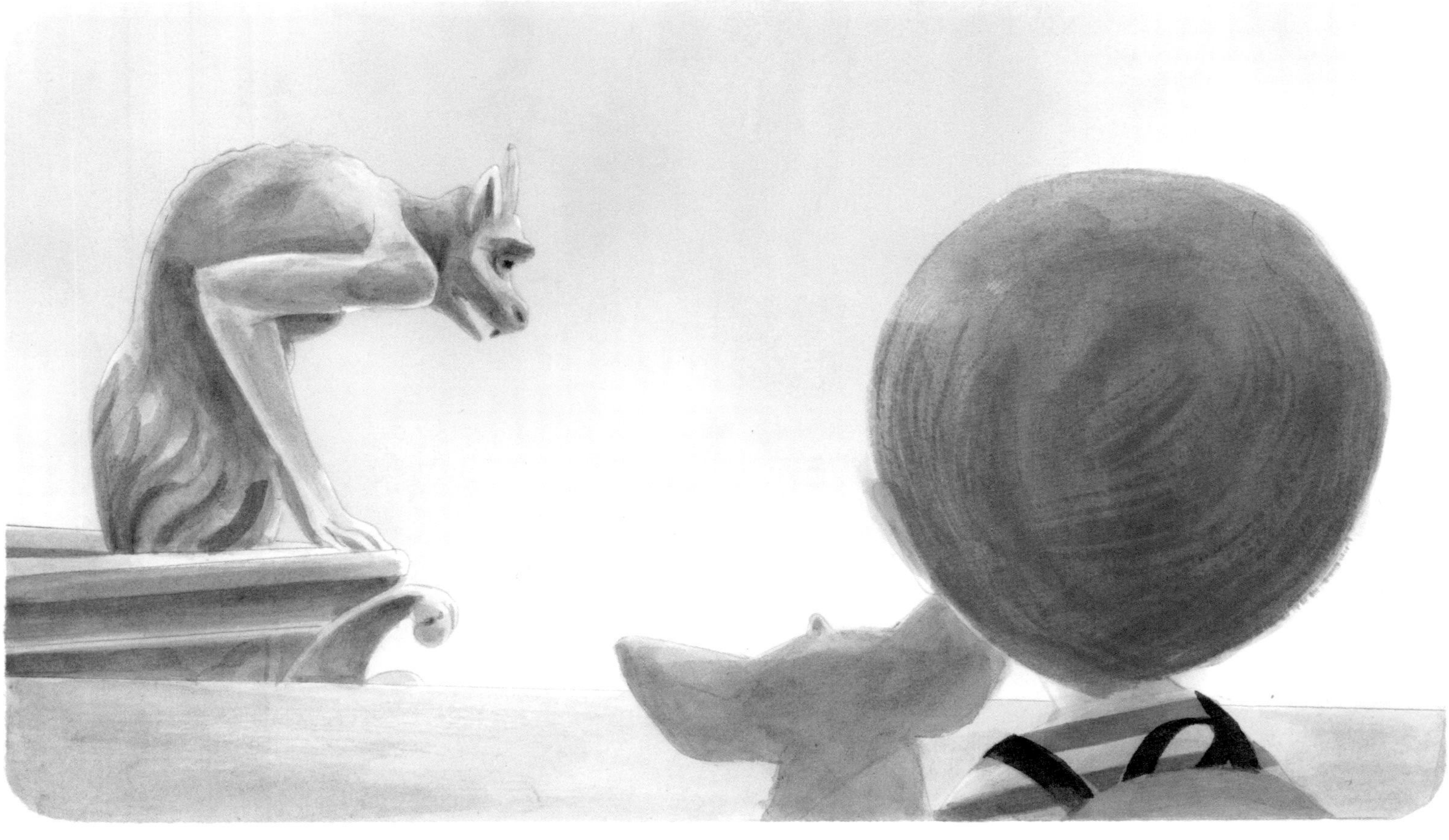

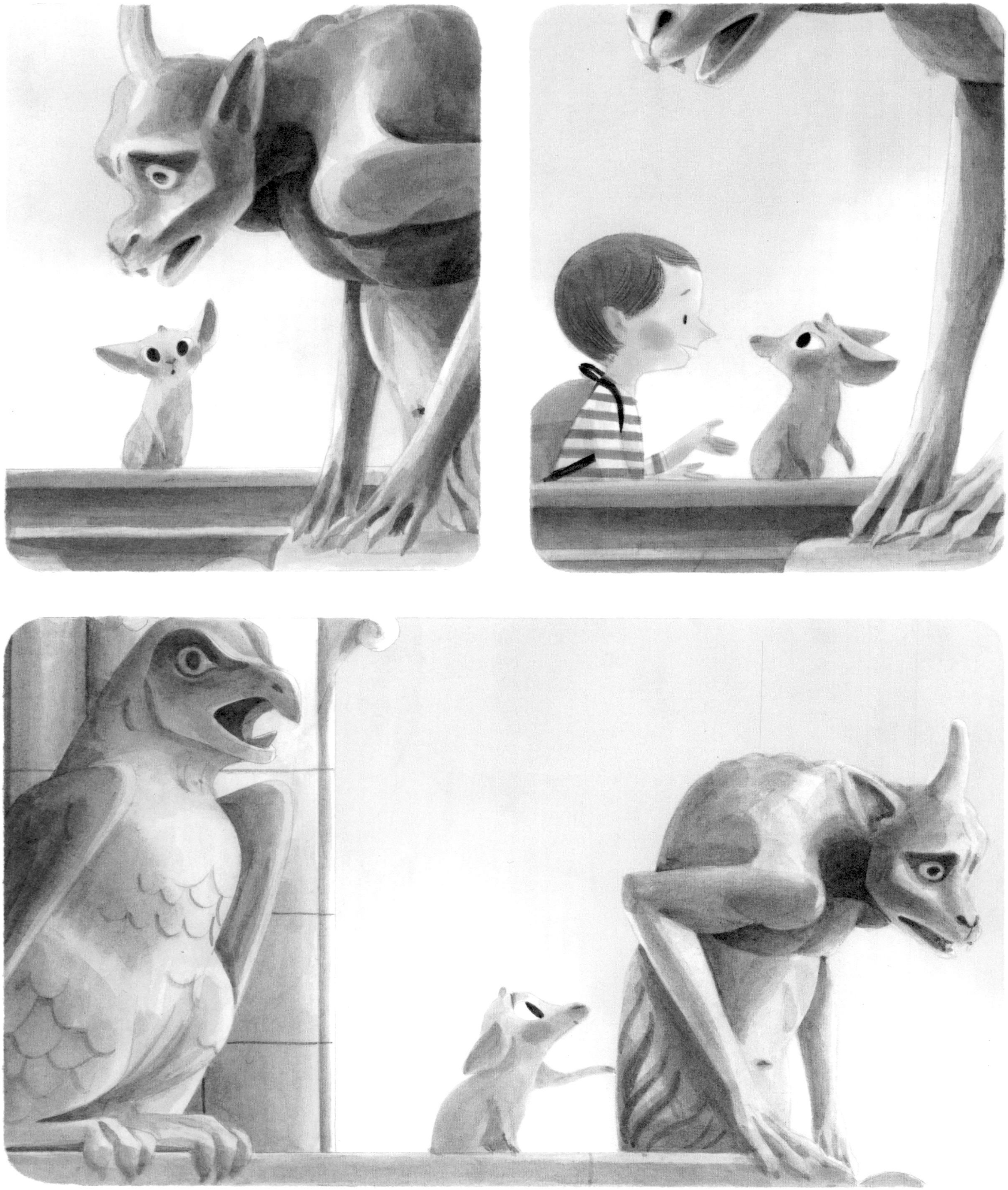

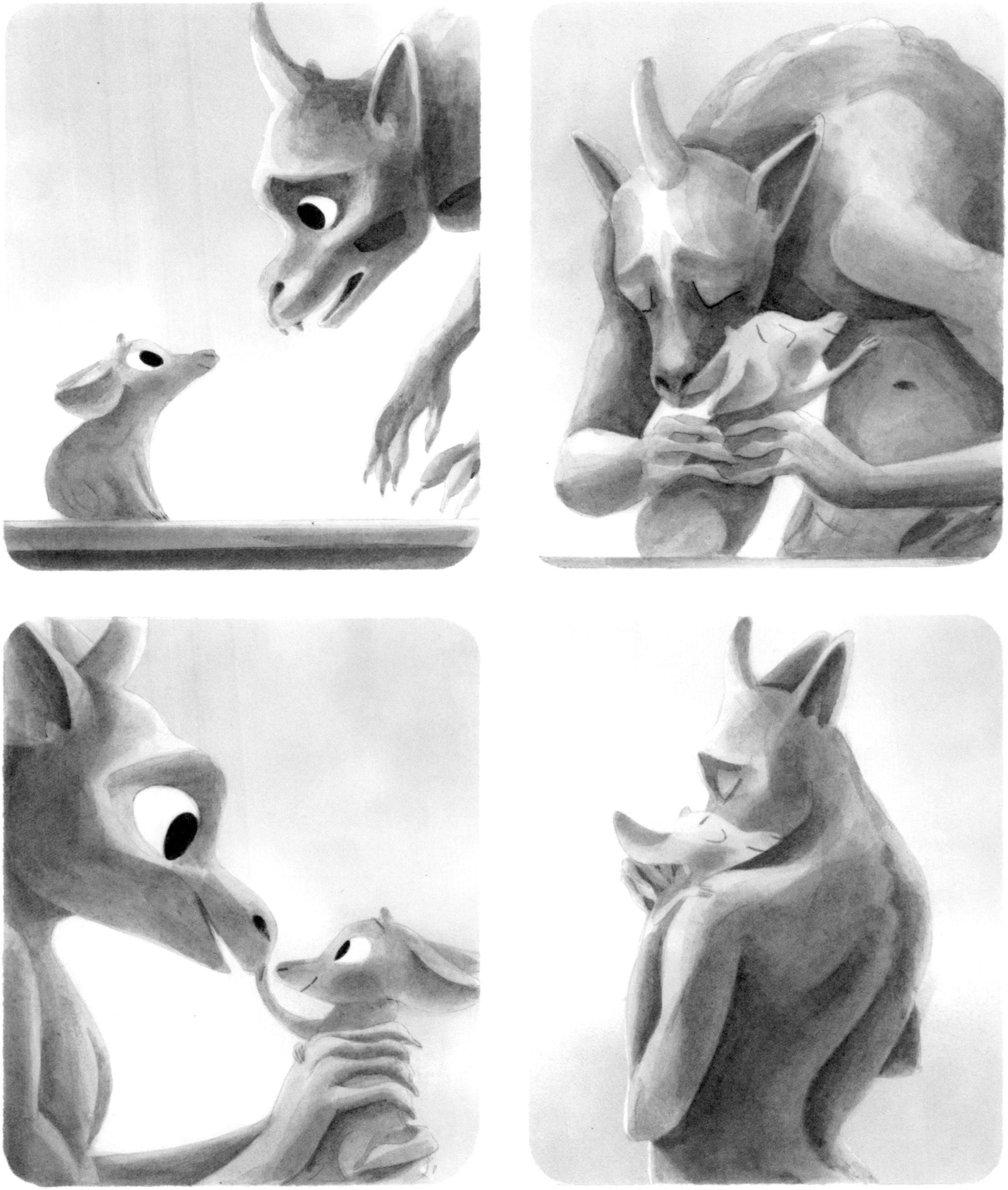

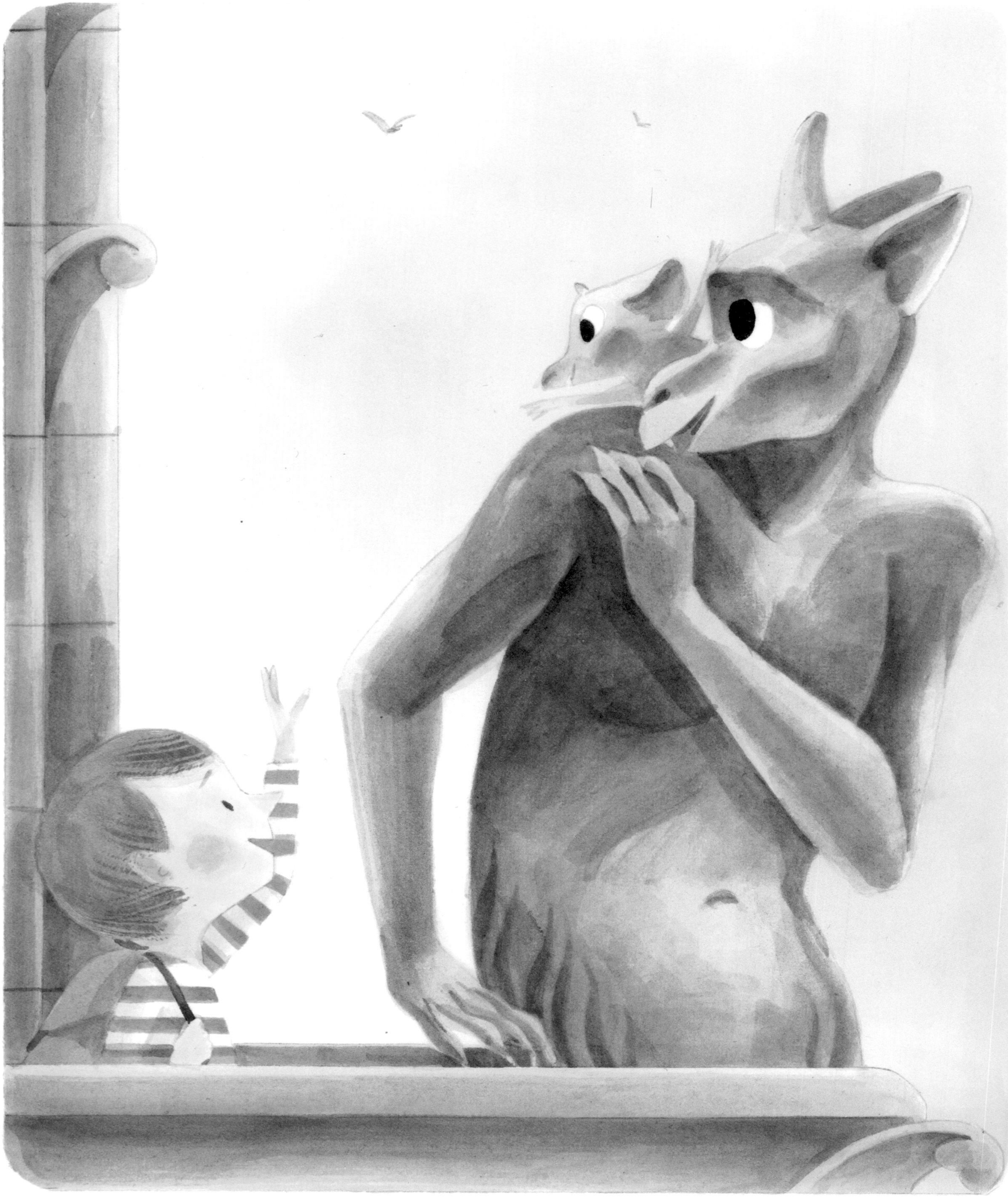

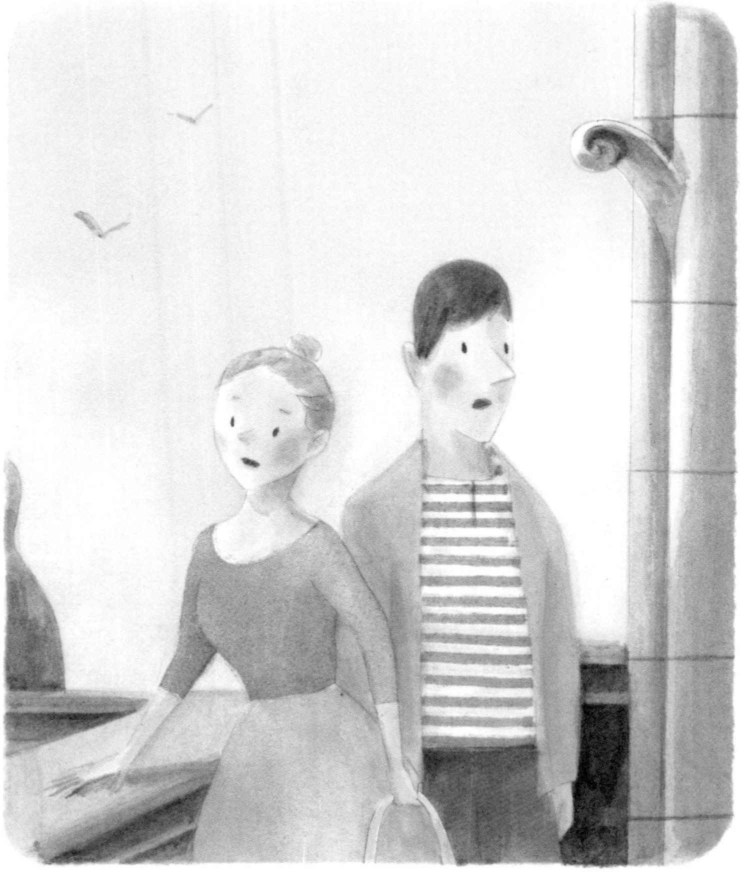

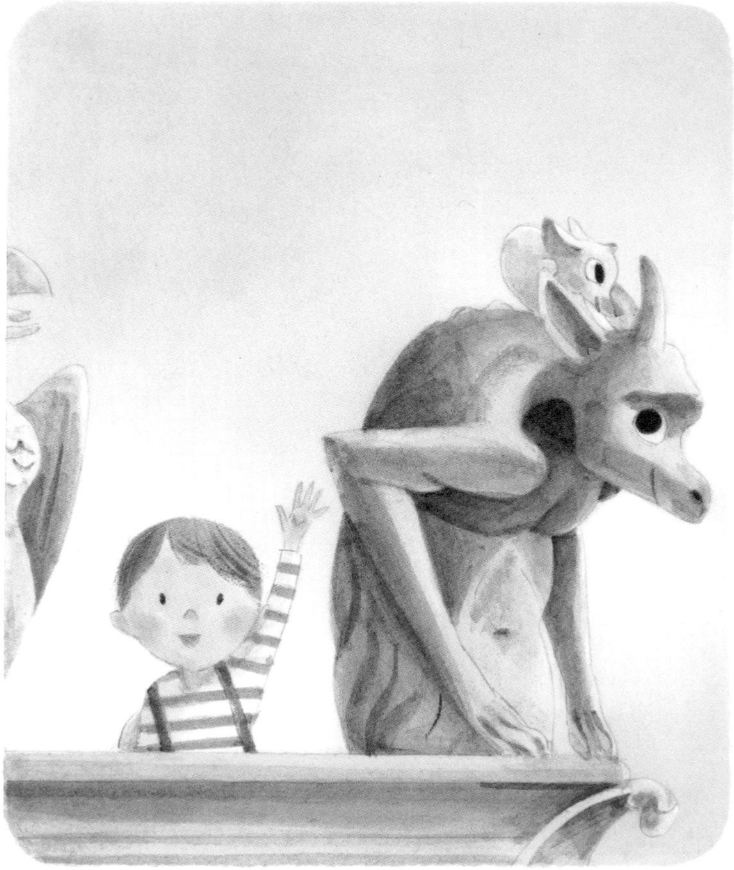

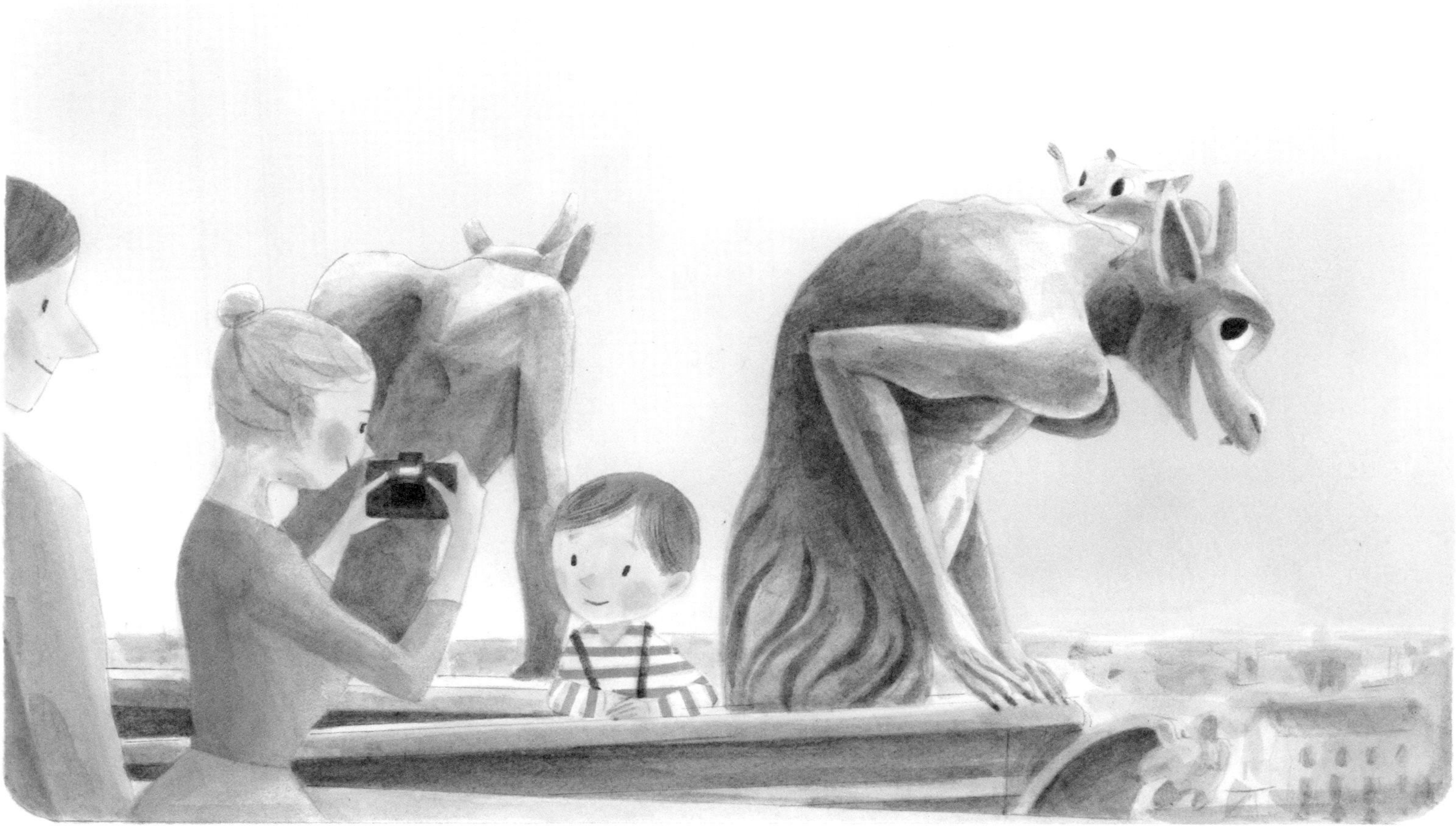

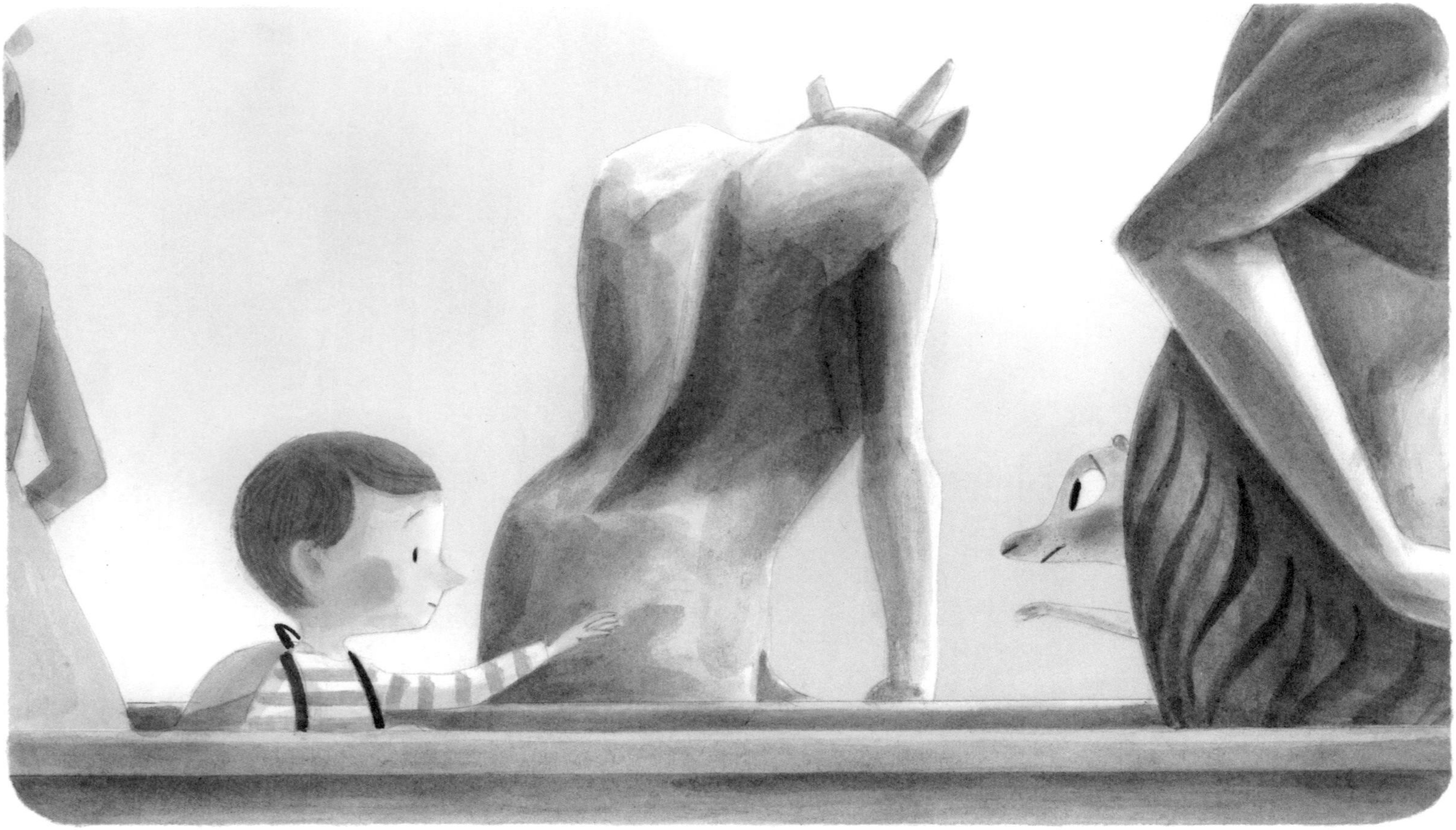

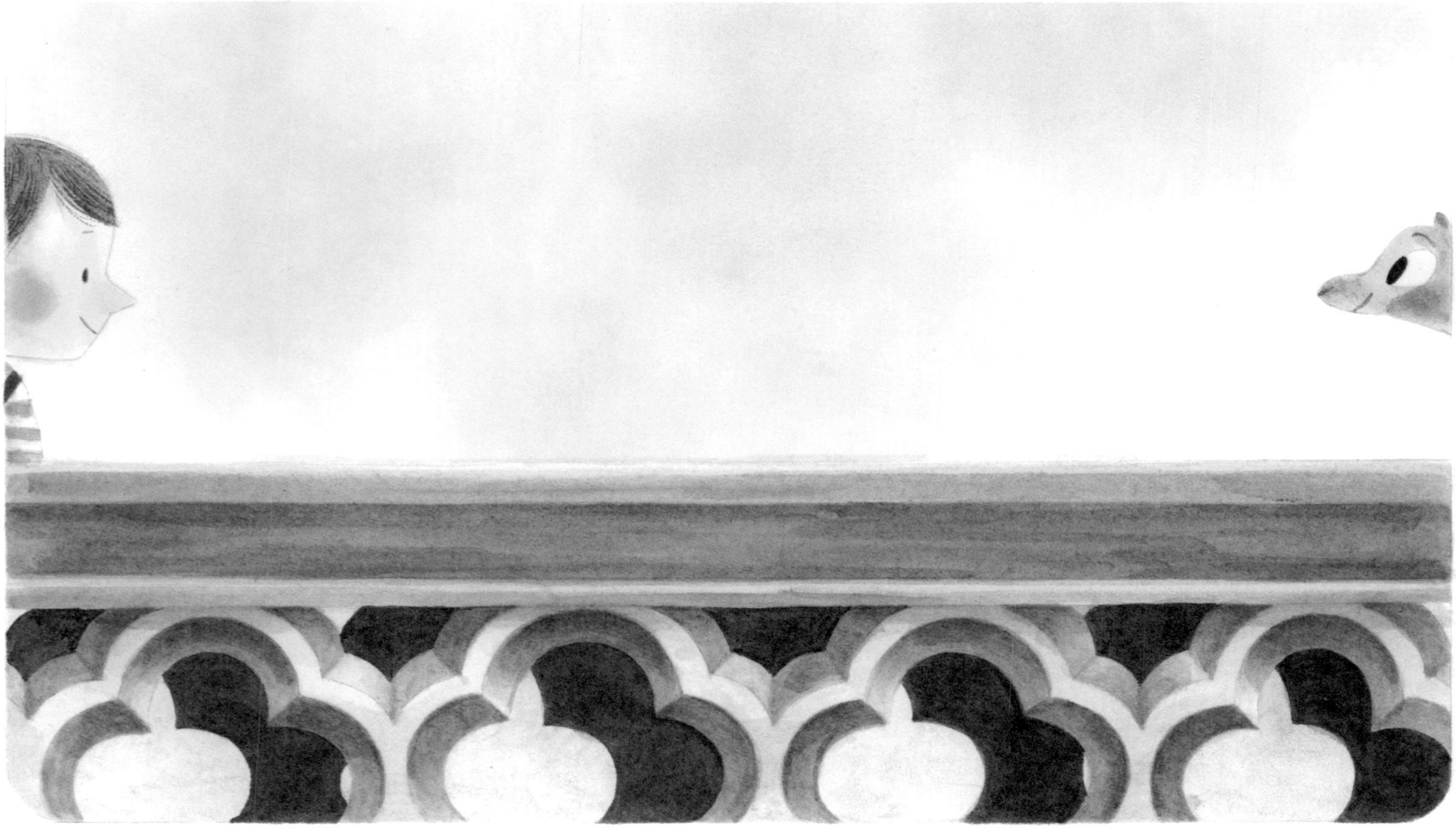

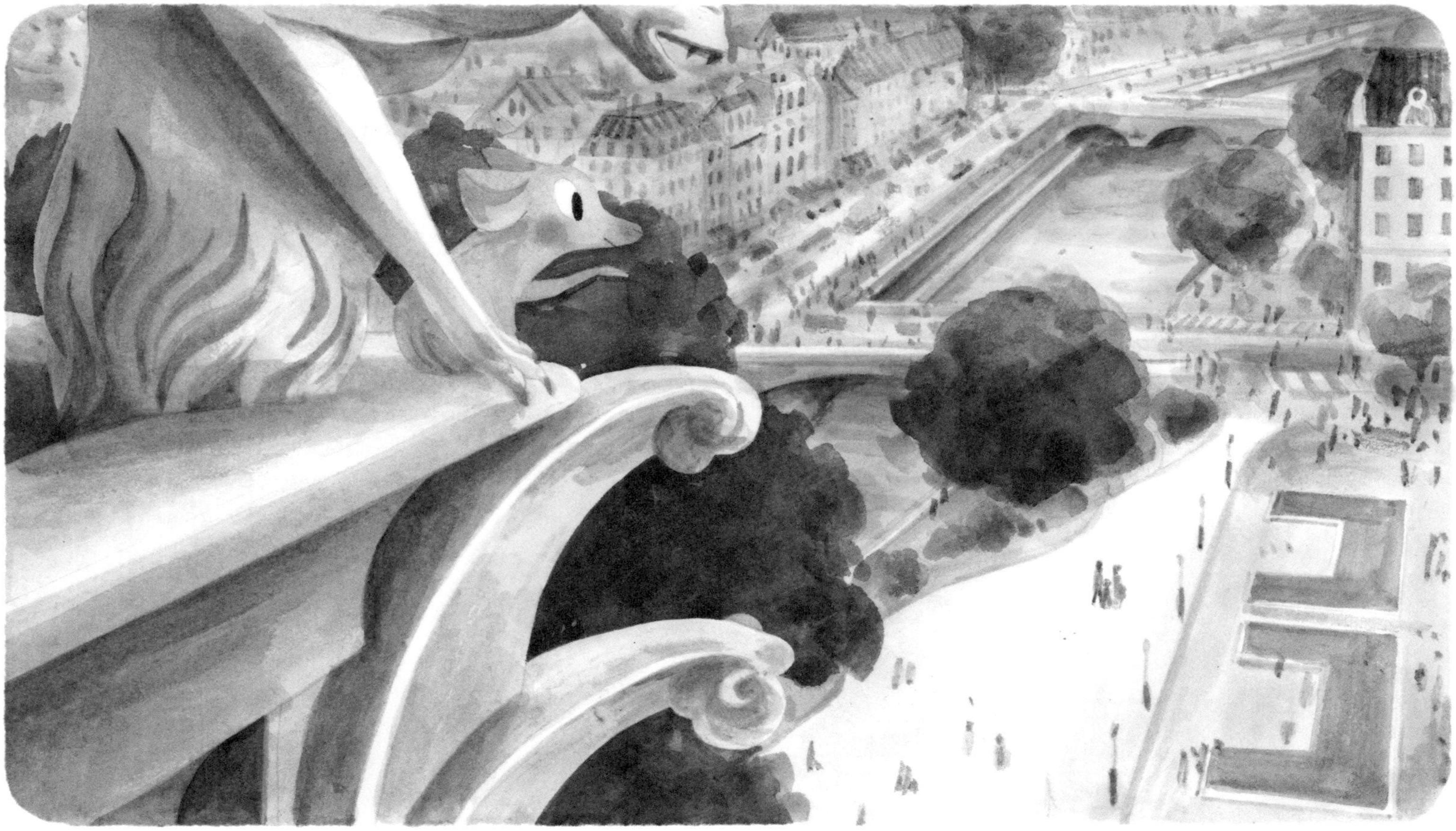

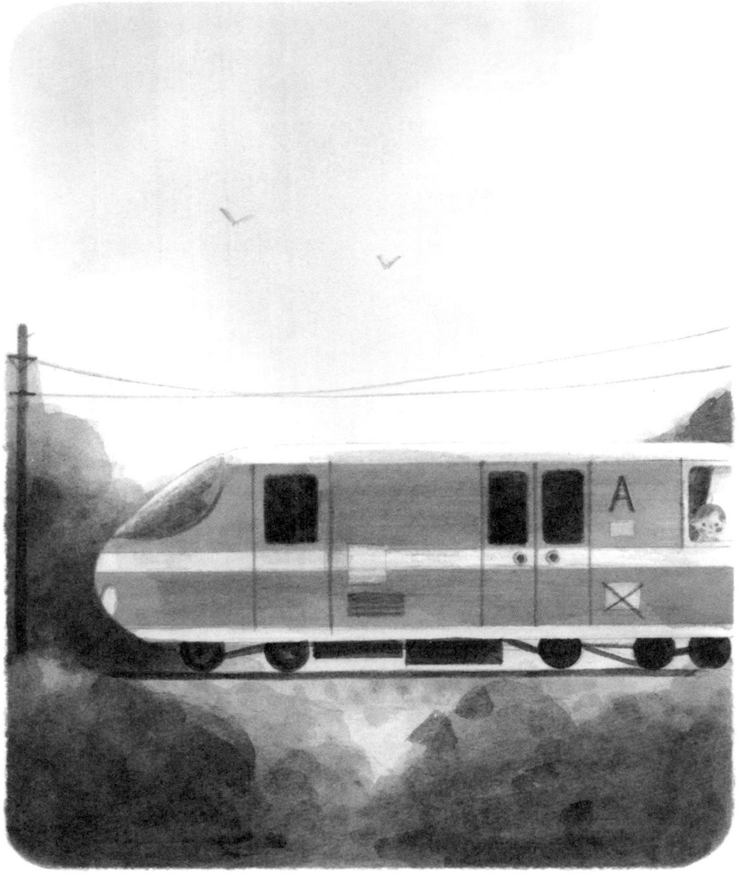
A

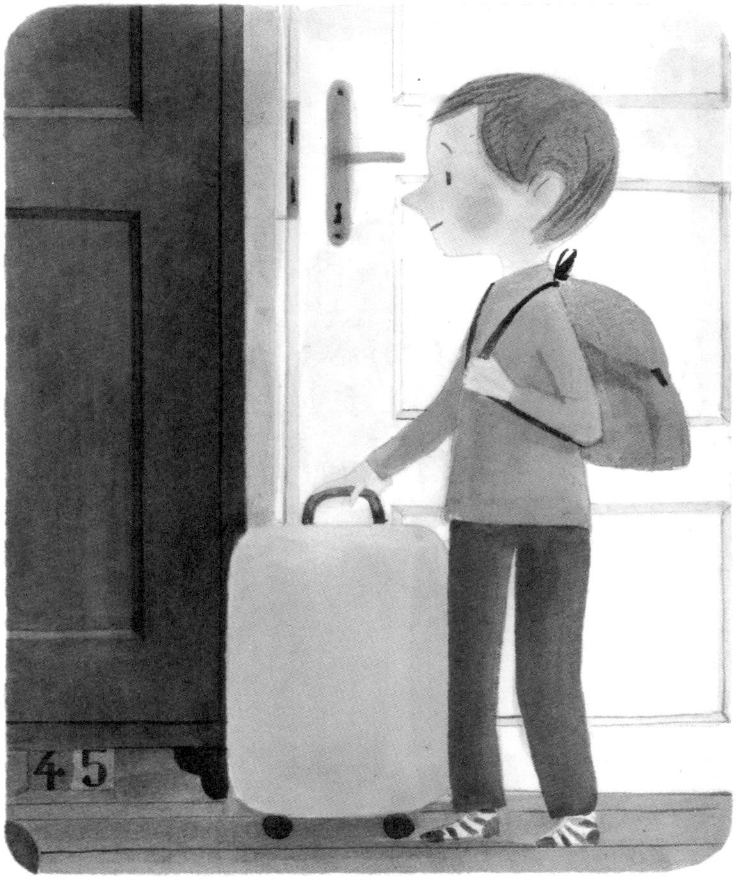
4 5

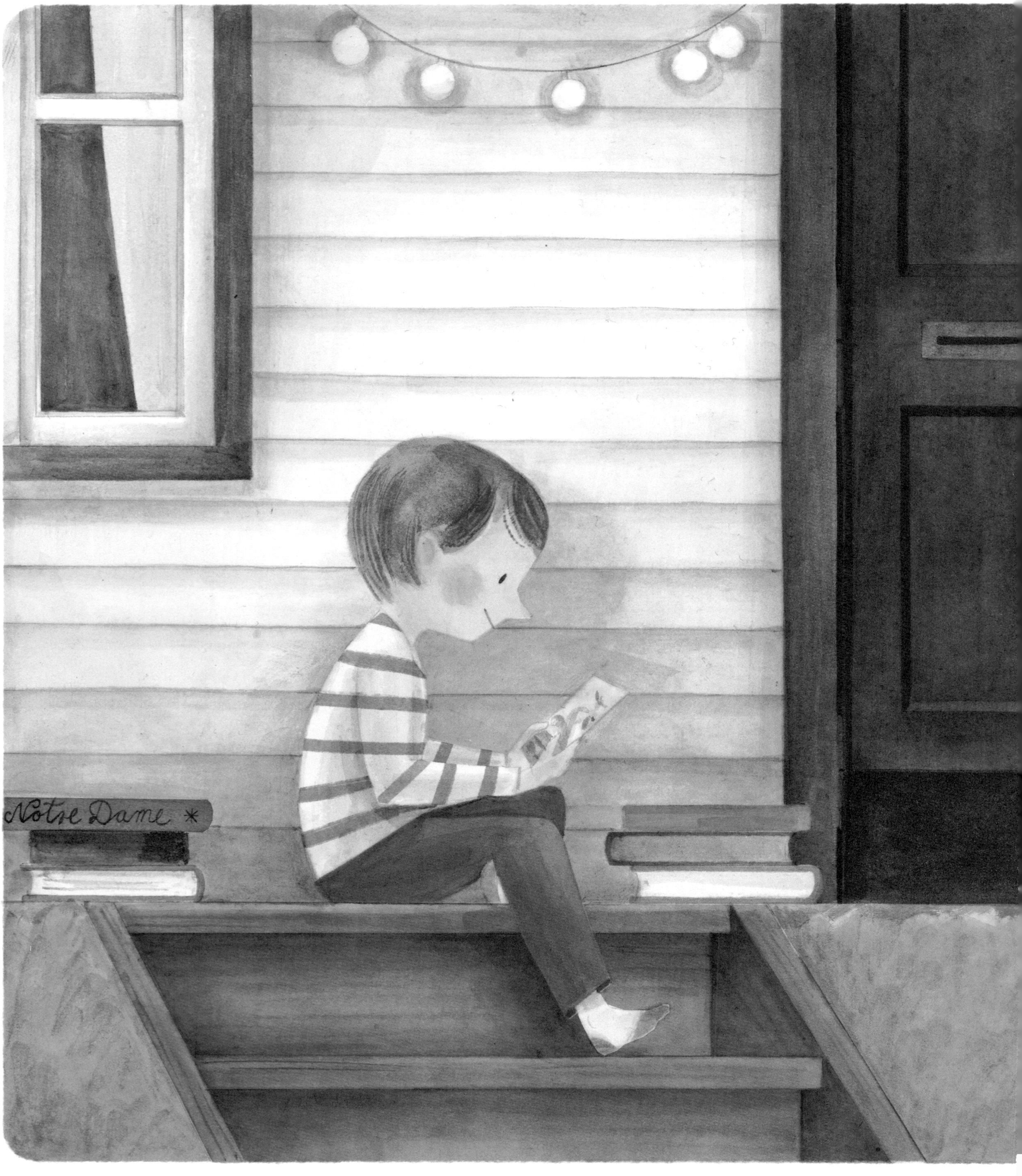
Notre Dame

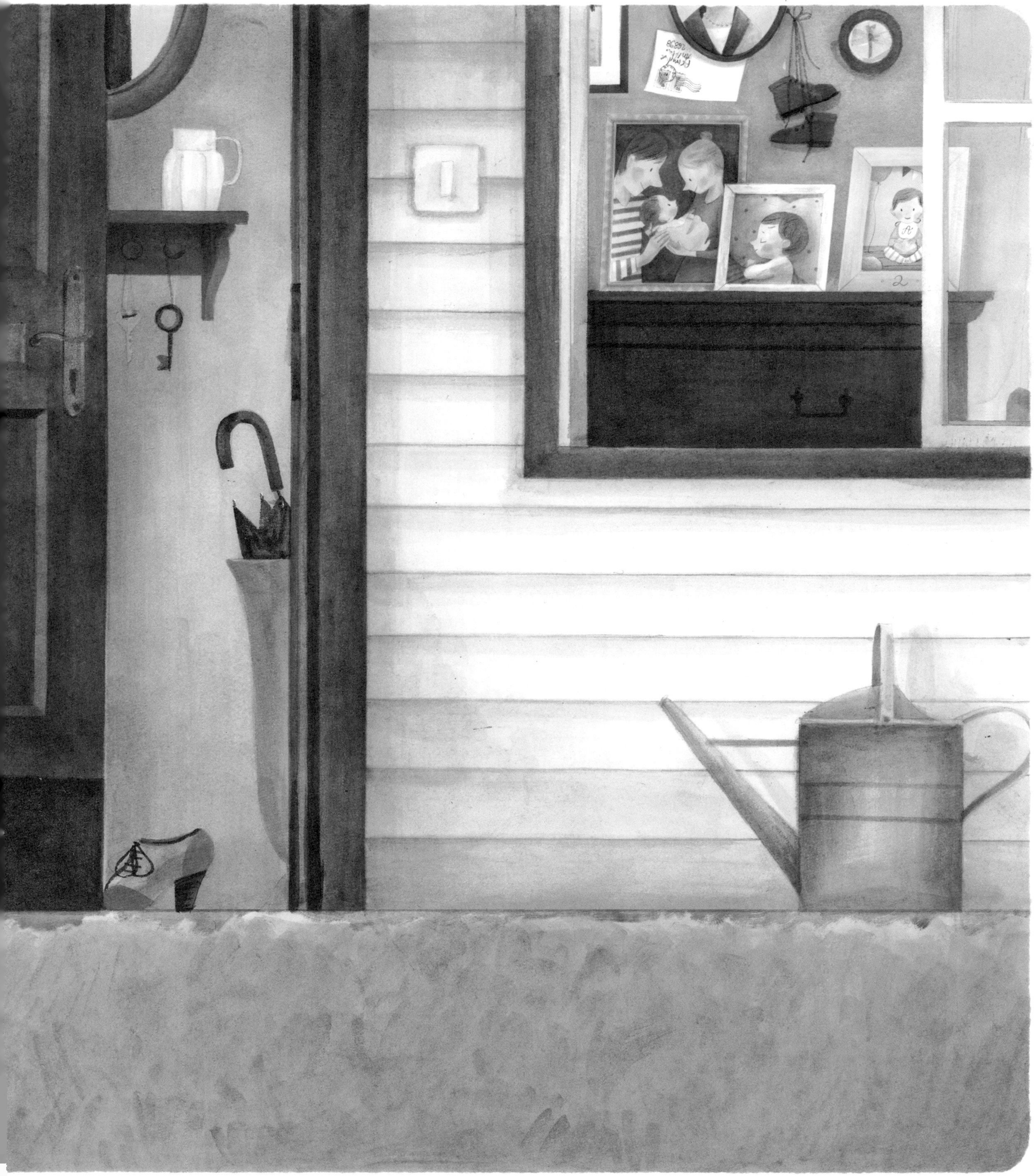

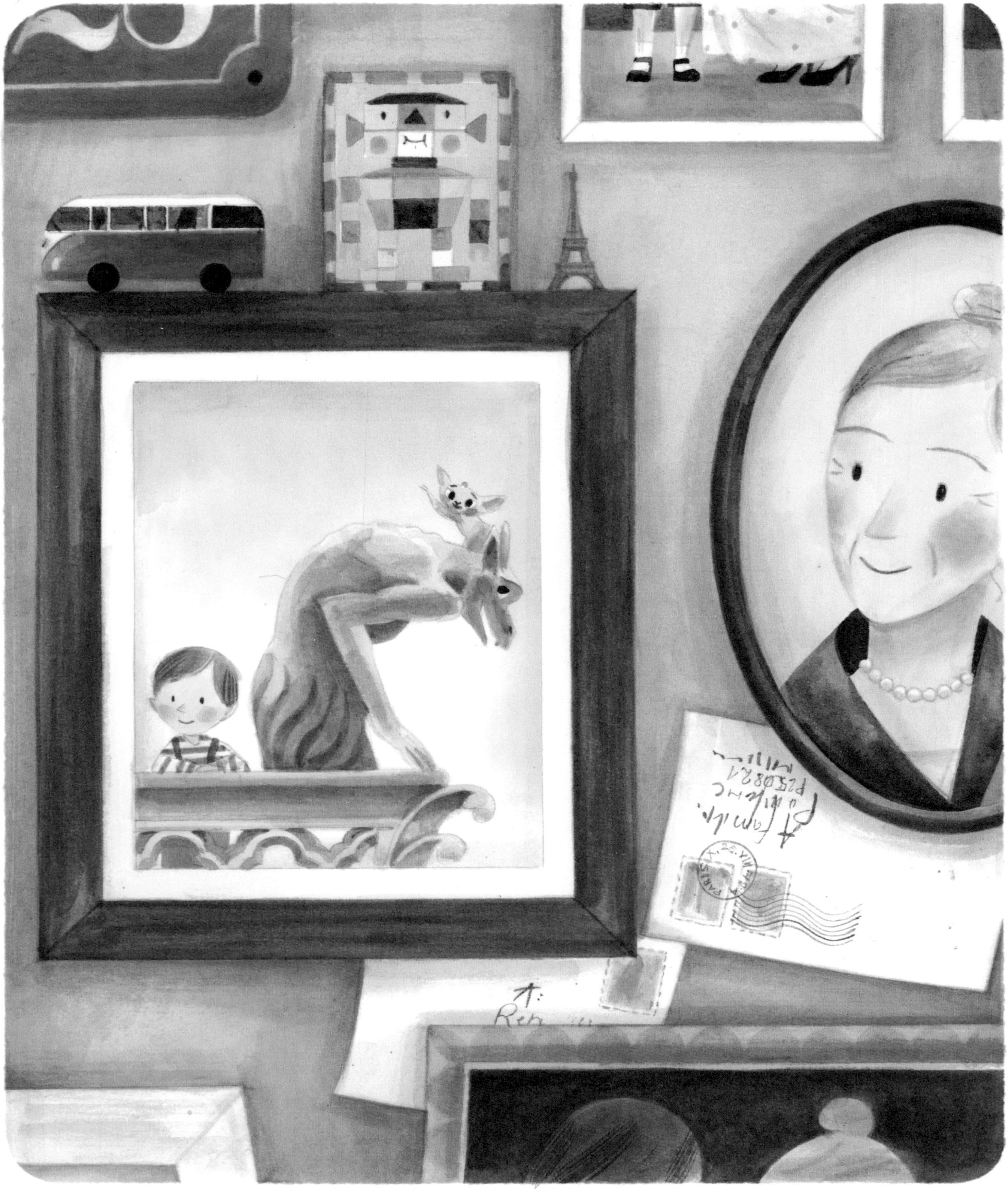